SO-AHH-806

SPACEMAN BLUES

A Tom Doherty Associates Book
New York

SPACEMAN BLUES

A Love Song

Brian Francis Slattery

This is a work of fiction. All of the characters, organizations, and events portrayed in this novel are either products of the author's imagination or are used fictitiously.

SPACEMAN BLUES: A LOVE SONG

Copyright © 2007 by Brian Francis Slattery

All rights reserved, including the right to reproduce this book, or portions thereof, in any form.

Edited by Liz Gorinsky

A Tor Book
Published by Tom Doherty Associates, LLC
175 Fifth Avenue
New York, NY 10010

www.tor.com

Tor® is a registered trademark of Tom Doherty Associates, LLC.

Library of Congress Cataloging-in-Publication Data

Slattery, Brian Francis.
    Spaceman blues: a love song / Brian Francis Slattery.—1st ed.
        p.   cm.
    "A Tom Doherty Associates Book."
    ISBN-13: 978-0-7653-1610-3 (hardcover)
    ISBN-10 : 0-7653-1610-2 (hardcover)
    ISBN-13: 978-0-7653-1614-1 (pbk.)
    ISBN-10: 0-7653-1614-5 (pbk.)
    I. Title.
    PS3619.L375S63   2007
    813'.6—dc22

                                          2007009543

First Edition: August 2007

Printed in the United States of America

0   9   8   7   6   5   4   3   2   1

SPACEMAN BLUES

CHAPTER 1

In Which a Man Disappears, and Several Parties Are Held

 The Last Hurrah

It is his last day, and by six in the morning he is already drinking, drinking and shot up, eyes frantic, limbs flailing like he's ready to explode. At seven he is on the wasted docks across from Manhattan starting fights with the winos and the mechanics; by eight thirty he's up in Washington Heights playing dominoes on a fire hydrant some kids are getting ready to crack open with a sledgehammer because it's so damn hot and the Hudson's so dirty and the ocean is too far away. By noon he's been thrown out of thirteen bars. He gets hit by a bus, gets drunk again with some boys in Spanish Harlem bobbing to bachata out of a static-ridden radio. The afternoon he spends smoking sweet tobacco and watching old movies in Arabic with the Egyptians in Astoria. He kisses Daoud's hand in Egypt Café, whispers something in his ear; then he rides the G back into Brooklyn, hops trains to Brighton Beach, where it's getting dark and the families are getting ready to go home. The men on the boardwalk totter with vodka, chase women, and eat boiled eggs, and he goes from club to club to tell the Russian Mafia he's leaving, he won't bother them anymore. By dark he is face-up on the pier at Coney Island, watching the first suns flare in the sky, the first stars of summer, out for that rare time when the humidity breaks and all is quiet, like the city is taking a breath, swelling the land under it, diverting water in the river and the bay to places farther out, deeper places; then it exhales, and all that was displaced returns, all that was disturbed tilts back into place, settles, grows quiet. And then, Manuel Rodrigo de Guzmán González vanishes. Poof.

For twenty-six hours, nobody knows he's gone. Everybody thinks he's with someone else, like the time he went to the Philippines and everyone thought he was in Jersey. He never answers his telephone anyway, they say. He tells people to call so he can let it ring twenty, thirty times. He has a phone from the sixties with a fire alarm bell on it; it helps him get to sleep.

Then his apartment explodes, blows apart the outside wall and rains bricks, plaster, timber and glass, burnt paper, shredded clothes in the street, but leaves the rest of the building standing, untouched. The news spreads in a widening circle of shock, people are talking about it up and down the street, voices crackle across the air and over wires. He's gone, he's gone, it goes in letters, in words flashing across flickering screens, it is written by planes in the sky. It spreads from the city and moves to the end of Long Island, into New Jersey, Connecticut, upstate, across New England; it moves across the continent over the miles of thrashing grain, the ragged heights of the Rockies, down into the deserts and dense forests and to the opposite shore, where men hear it on shortwave radios at the place where the Mexican border falls into the Pacific Ocean, and the waves roll in gigantic and break against the rocks and sand with a force that ensures compliance. It passes along the piers of Eastern Europe, syllables slipped between knife points and rusting rifles; on the shores of Angola they wail at the ocean, beat their feet into the sand, turn back toward crumbling cities. The news burns bodies in the Bronx, things are cast adrift in the deep water of the East River, people depart into the sky, there are meetings in drainage systems, encoded signals broadcast in the flight patterns of birds, machines stir, motors grind into action at frequencies only subterranean people can feel. And people begin to congregate in the places that Manuel loved. They want to know what happened, they want to understand, but being the kind of people they are, all that wanting turns into partying. In Astoria, Egypt Café is jammed to the ceiling, people walk over other people to get inside, they spill out onto the street in front of the Laundromat, they raid the delis and liquor stores and close down Steinway, they make a party so big that the police see it and just throw up their hands, set up roadblocks, join in when they get off duty. At the Maritime Lounge in Red Hook, some Congolese soukous band appears out of nowhere and plays for two days straight, they have to coat their fingers with glue in between numbers to keep the skin on, and the crowd crashes in and chokes on seven different kinds of smoke and laughter, they pour beer and whiskey all over each other and dance to break floorboards. The place runs out of alcohol after eighteen hours but people keep bringing in more, they toast Manuel again and again, wish to God you were still here. They end up in the water of the harbor, holding their drinks high and setting them on fire until the end of the second day rolls by and they go to sleep in the street, they crawl home in a blind drag. They pass out in subway cars, they wake up feeling like their brains are cut in half. They go home in pairs and wake up naked with each other, their furniture upended, dishes broken, sheets ripped into long shreds, clothes plastered somehow to the ceiling. And Wendell Apogee weaves home alone in the dark, through the cheers and the falling confetti, the flash and bang of fireworks, all the way back from Red Hook to Astoria where the crowd is dead from dancing; and he goes to his apartment, opens the window to the stifling summer air, drenches himself in freezing water, and then falls on the floor and cries.

 Our Hero

He wakes up the next morning escaping from heat-troubled sleep, thrashing to life in the sun that's already baking concrete, melting the antennae of cars. Downstairs he can hear his old landlord moaning, a World War Two refugee who will spend the day spitting at his fat dog and sweltering into his velour armchair. In the apartments around him, people have their shirts off and are hanging out the window, running soaked towels over their arms. Two women lounge in bikinis on the roof with a radio playing a melted Cuban cassette, they fan themselves with newspapers and fling Spanish curses to the boys on the fire escape who whistle at them between dousing swigs of frozen malt liquor from frosted plastic bottles. All across the city it is like this, you feel heat flow from every surface and multiply, push under your skin and cook you off your bones. People crawl into their blasting air conditioners, sixteen of the elderly pass away, vagrants and runaways wade into the filth of the East River, kids break open Siamese plugs on buildings and lie in the gutter in their underwear, letting the water crest over them, over their hands and hot faces, knowing they'd felt cold once, oh, not six months ago; but the heat is like the flu: three days into it and you can't remember what it was like to be well.

For the nascent Church of Panic, it's part of its mythology. In robes of black and white, its members hover four inches over the pavement, gliding in formations of three up and down major thoroughfares. They jostle the quality on Lexington south of 96th, pass through the South Americans on Brooklyn's Fifth Avenue, collide with Dominicans at Broadway and 160th. The heat is a portent, they say, a sign of the chaos to come. We are the Prophets of Fear, the Angels of Paralysis. Begin stockpiling weapons now. They seem serious.

The authorities are investigating the explosion in Manuel's apartment, collecting testimony from witnesses and neighbors. There was first a warping sound, they say, a rush of air that rattled windows and stripped hats from heads. Then the fire shot straight out in a column of wide flame that broke against the building across the street, rolled across its face, and was gone. Neighbors who peered into the hallway afterward saw smoke snaking from under the door, through the keyhole. Now the police are calling every name they can find in what remains of Manuel's things. Come to his apartment for an interview, they say. It will not be like a wake. But it is.

The door to Manuel's apartment is charred around the edges; shocks of black streak from the corners, through the locks. Inside, all is ruin. The couch is burned down to melted springs and withered struts, chairs and tables are blown into shadows. The walls are tortured plaster, fused wiring, the appliances a pile of slag. And at the apartment's edge, nothing: just the open air above the street, the last step to suicide laced by police tape, framed by swinging cables, nails, burnt walls, silent pigeons.

"Mr. . . . Apogee?"

"Yes? . . ."

"Inspector Herman Trout. My partner, Lenny Salmon. We recognized you from this." The policeman holds up a bubbled, half-melted photograph, a close shot of Wendell and Manuel, their faces smiling, almost cheek to cheek, arms around each other's backs. The angle of Wendell's shoulder tells you that he took the picture himself, holding the camera out in front of him while the two of them squinted into the flash. In the background, throbbing lights, raving hands reaching toward them.

"Where did you find it?"

"In the oven with his birth certificate," Salmon says. "Mr. Apogee—"

"—Wendell."

"Wendell." Salmon says. "Would you say that you were friends with Mr. González?"

"I . . . friends? Yes, we were . . . very good friends, we . . ."

"Would you say that you were familiar with his friends?" Trout says.

"Yes. Well . . . some of them, he had so many friends . . ."

"Mr. Apogee," Trout says. "We have compiled a list of over eighty-seven people who describe themselves as close, personal friends of Mr. González. Now here is the conundrum: none of them can say where he went."

"They have some interesting ideas," Salmon says.

"A certain Lucas Henderson . . ." Trout licks his thumb, flips through the pages of a small notebook. "Yes, here, told us that quote Manuel's vanishing is not a disappearance, it is an apotheosis unquote. . . ."

"Some of them said he went to Hungary. Or Mars."

"Or Senegal."

"Something about running Soviet-era weaponry to African revolutionaries."

"Money laundering for certain government officials in Turkmenistan, taking a percentage of their profits in the Central Asian opiate trade, which appears to be quite lucrative."

"We've heard a lot of stories today, Wendell. Want to know how most of them end?"

"... I don't know, do you think I want to know this?"

"They told us to ask *you* where he went."

"... what?"

"That's right."

"..."

"..."

"But I have no idea where he is."

"They said you would know. They said he told you everything. They said you knew him best."

The night before his last day, Manuel visited Wendell at two in the morning, swung hand over hand along the power lines to his building and slid through the open window. He must have watched Wendell sleep for an hour. He walked around the bed, put a hand on the shoulder that pushed up a ridge under the covers, and sobbed until Wendell woke and put his arms out to comfort him. Manuel told him many things that night, piteous and cruel, but it was nonsense, Wendell understood so little of it, he just wanted his baby to be calm, to roll into his arms and go to sleep. It's too much, Manuel said. I'm going, I'm leaving everything and going.

You can't leave me, Wendell said. Don't go away from me. And he locked his arms around Manuel's chest and Manuel slowed, as if coming to some sort of peace. He said he would not go, he seemed to rest; but he must have changed his mind again, or maybe he was lying, because he was gone now, gone leaving Wendell's hands clutching at air, frayed nerves buzzing, looking for their ends.

"I thought I knew him. I really did," Wendell says.

He walks back to the subway in a heat like the sun is coming closer, a tendril of nuclear fire reaching out to lick the surface of this hapless planet, run a scorch mark a thousand miles across a continent, string up a chain of smoking cities, ashen farmlands. At the corner near the subway stop, men and women have gathered, they're shielding their eyes with their hands. One of them saw something up in the sky and they're talking about it. It was like a jellyfish, all eyes and hungry limbs, writhing in the air. A creature of heat stroke, someone says. The squiggling image of the sun burning into your retina. And this from a trio of priests of the Church of Panic: it begins.

There are twenty-six messages on Wendell's machine when he gets home. The first is from Lucas Henderson: he is having a party that night for Witnesses to the Ascension of González, bring etcetera. Then twenty-three more from various friends of Manuel, informing him of said party, love it if you'd come, be great to see you, how are you holding up, need to stick together. We all miss him, really we do. Then a long rambling message from the policeman he just talked to, Inspector Salmon. Sorry if his questions were upsetting, he could tell they made Wendell uncomfortable. He wanted to make clear that nobody considered Wendell guilty of anything and they wanted to keep in touch, please call if he found anything or just wanted to talk about it. A cough. Then message twenty-six: a woman's voice drenched in a Spanish accent, crackling with distance.

"The phone is about to ring," she says. "Do not answer it."

The phone rings.

"Do not answer it."

Wendell does, a hello . . . ? that pinches down his throat and comes out meek and scared. At first, nothing answers, there is only the sound of his own breath and the ambient noise of the street filtering through the receiver; but then a hiss emerges from this, a hiss that widens as if something is approaching, voices become distinct from one another, the sounds of men, women, and children, and at first it seems as if they are whispering, no, they're chanting, but then Wendell can hear it for sure: they're screaming, screaming above the keen of engines and now a howl that dives down from the sky and tears the earth apart. A giant hand wriggles through the phone line and strains through the sieve of the receiver to enter Wendell's head, push its fingers into his brain, and the phone slips from his grasp, swings on the cord and smacks against the floor; and Wendell teeters like his feet are on a fulcrum, and the ground has rotated to accept him. Lights out.

 Wendell's Dream #1

The road that bends and angles up from Huehuetenango in Guatemala and hangs along the edge of the long valley in the ruddy Cuchumantanes ends at Todos Santos, a steep cluster of layered houses, cobbled passages, and muddy alleys where the people still wear Maya garb and the families still feel the spaces from all those deaths, deaths in the civil war not long ago when they gathered men, women, and children and shot them in the square, chased them up into the hills and shot them there; it is a place of half-finished buildings, of stray unspayed dogs and a terraced plaza where the men in red pants and shirts of many colors lean against the railings and exchange words, and the market every Saturday brings them in from the hills with vegetables, pigs on leashes, hinges, and foggy cassettes of ranchero and electric ballads. In the evening, when the shadow of one side of the valley crawls up the other and the lights flicker on in the street, and people strike candles in their houses and the music starts up in the evangelical church, bass and accordion and tuba, and the houses filter buzzing marimba music through portable radios into the darkness, it is mournful, it is joyful, it winds around the end of the day and brings rest.

Manuel has fled to this place and built a house on one of its streets, a house that has one story when it starts, but stretches to three as the land falls away beneath it. He's in the panadería overlooking the square during the day, drinking instant coffee with sweet rolls, and at night he stands in the street, speaking in slow tones with other men and drinking Gallo beer from long, brown bottles, watching kids play with bicycle tires, people packing things out of town in bundles lashed to their heads, while in the plaza a tourist gets the most expensive shoeshine the town has ever seen. And he is there where the road ends at the church when the bus from Huehuetenango pulls in, coughing diesel and shaking off dust. Farmers and artisans descend; then Wendell, who has dirt on his hands and grime in his hair, and has brought nothing with him.

"I knew you'd be able to find me," Manuel says.

"Don't leave me again."

"Then stay here."

And Wendell moves forward and embraces him. Manuel puts his lips to Wendell's ear and repeats it: stay, stay; and Wendell's hands move on Manuel's shoulders: I will, I will. . . .

 ## Yellow Skis

Lucas Henderson labors down Lorraine Street in Red Hook, thinking. Once the neighborhood was rowdy with sailors, dark ships heaving on the water, piers creaking against the rocks, prostitutes, fights, and vomit. There were factory fires and parties, longshoremen shooting each other over illegal booze, floating hotels and movies on the playground. Then the piers began to close, the city bored a tunnel, flung a highway through the neighborhood, severed it from the mainland. Up rose the cross-shaped projects while the houses slumped on the cobbled streets, they put in only the streetlights they had to, made days and nights of boredom and violence, of stepping over corpses in the doorway. Now the artists have moved in closer to the water, the upwardly mobile followed with their giant stores and condominiums, put in a ferry to Manhattan in the places where sailors kissed their girls and fell drunk in the water. So many plans, unready for the winds that would tear down houses, the coming firestorms. The newspapers and magazines all say the neighborhood's changed forever now, they're holding funerals for the Red Hook that was. But along the streets of fried-chicken places and Laundromats, check-cashing stores and community centers, merengue and hip-hop bouncing off the sidewalk, the people know that the papers aren't talking about them. Maybe closer to the water, where there's a wine shop, new paint jobs, European cars. But here there are still soccer games in the wide parks by the pool, here they pull Central America out of the ground and you can eat pupusas and tacos with shards of coconut and a bottle of Jarritos while the men who work night construction jobs tear across the field in striped jerseys. Near the projects, the old sit on benches and smoke, talk of nothing; the boys in long shorts and baseball caps mob the sidewalk, drink off the heat with forties. Bless you my sons, Lucas says. In his arms and on his back he bears the weight of bottles and bottles of whiskey and vodka, a few jugs of wine, so that the Witnesses to the Ascension, aka Manuel's friends, may be merry.

Lucas was born into the Lunar Temple, a group of Americans, most from the Southwest, who believed that the Moon was a part of the Earth that was broken off in an ancient cataclysm, and that humans were devolved from more pure creatures who now lived in vast, spiral cities below the satellite's surface. These beings were building monstrous engines two hundred miles across on the dark side of the Moon that, on the Day of Joining, they would use to bring the Moon hurtling back to Earth. The Lunar Temple calculated that the first point of contact between the two bodies would be one of the peaks in the upper range of the Sierra Nevadas; the Founder built their compound there so that, on the Day, they could tilt their heads skyward and be the first to kiss the heavenly body and welcome it home. The first twelve years of Lucas's life were spent eating, sleeping, and, in the last few months, mating in that place, watching from his window every night while the first generation of the Temple wandered around in the yard staring up at the Moon, mouths open like chickens in the rain.

Two months before Lucas's thirteenth birthday, as he was about to make it with the Founder's fifteenth daughter, a great light descended from above. Alarms sounded, people shouted, the Day was at hand, and everyone clustered within the white circle the Founder had drawn at the summit and assumed the position they had drilled: back straight, up on tiptoes, neck craned, lips puckered. But the approaching light and noise turned out to be an FBI helicopter, followed by several more carrying men in riot gear who arrested the Founder on charges of illegal arms possession, corrupting minors, and aggravated assault. The compound was razed; in its place the state built four wooden benches and a concession stand.

Of the second half of his life, the years after deprogramming and before Red Hook, Lucas says nothing. They are incidental to the foundation of my personality, which has been cheated the sweet oblivion of apocalypse, he has said. He has trouble getting dates. Women back away, hands out, defensive. But this matters little, for Lucas knows how to throw parties.

"In every second, mass death, death by the millions, has

been averted by the slightest margin," he explains. "For this reason, it is important that every party be of the highest quality."

So he trudges down Lorraine on his way to Van Brunt, bottles clinking, the boys with the forties smirking and raising their drinks to him. The cops beep their horns once or twice, they know him and how cooperative he is with authorities when his celebrations get out of hand: in his kitchen is a baseball bat that he wields with what he calls the Hand of the Righteous.

Diane is waiting for him on the steps; she has pulled up her shirt with one hand and is palpating her stomach with the other.

"They're going to bust you, with all that booze," she says.

"Avaunt, harlot."

"Avaunt? Who talks like that? Where'd you go to high school?"

"Diane, I never attended high school."

Diane became prom queen after her three rivals, triplets, died in a boating accident on the lake near where she grew up. One of them had been waterskiing: they found a yellow shard of one of the skis flipping in the current a foot below the surface. One of them must have been driving the boat, but what the third one was doing, nobody could say for sure. Witnesses say the boat launched into the air, cut a high arc above the water that was traced by the tow line and skier, then plunged nose-first into the waves, dragging the skier down with it. Nobody is sure how the triplets got the boat to fly, but Diane remembers that all through the senior dance, while her boyfriend's hands sweated on her back, she kept thinking of that boat falling

427 feet through the cold black water, the first two triplets aboard, hands locked to the railing, eyes open, the third with her fingers curled around the handle of the line, legs splayed out behind her, following them down. It was suicide, she was sure of it: one of them had planned it, and when the other two realized what was happening, they accepted. Diane still thinks of those triplets now and again, there at the bottom of the glacier-scraped lake where the water never freezes, their boat resting on the ribs of old rotting barges, the long bodies of drowned Iroquois canoes, and below them all, the massive skeletons of giant lake trout that died before humans ever showed up.

Diane has five boyfriends, all of whom will be coming to the party. Four of them, Lázaro, Enrique, Fernando, and Rigoberto, are diminutive Ecuadorians who play on the same soccer team, the 101st Street Auto Depot Flyers, in the summer league in Central Park, even though they all live in Queens and do not work at the depot. They are capable of acrobatic tricks on the field and have never lost a game. Her fifth and most casual boyfriend is Masoud Azzi, a Lebanese man who flew fighter planes for the Syrian air force, then became a pacifist and moved to Astoria, where he lives two blocks closer to the subway than Wendell but pays a third of the rent, thanks to his familial connections. No broker's fee, either. When he is drunk on ouzo, Masoud likes to remind Wendell of this; then he practices yoga to prevent the onset of hangover. Diane loves all five of them the same, yes, her heart is big enough for that, but she loves Lucas the most and it is taking apart her internal organs; twice she has been hospitalized, near to death. Yet she tells Lucas nothing. Maybe Lucas can see it in her anyway, maybe he can't; if he can, he gives no sign, only the cold glance he reserves for all his friends.

"Either relieve me of some of my burden or step aside and let me pass," Lucas says. And she steps aside, but only by inches, so that accident might allow them to touch.

Blood on the Floor

One hundred years ago, Lucas's apartment was the workplace of Dr. Bernie, Butchery and Surgery. His living room was filled with meat, a thick curtain of slaughtered pigs suspended from hooks and draining, spinning when jostled, gathering flies. Dr. Bernie hung the hogs himself, butchered them on the floor. If you pushed through this wall of flesh, though, you'd come across a pristine white table where, using the same instruments he used on the hogs, Dr. Bernie stitched cuts, set limbs, lanced boils, popped eyes back in their sockets, performed amputations. He was shut down in 1910 by a corpulent, phlegmatic man from the new FDA, who deemed unsanitary the performing of surgery amid food meant for consumption. Dr. Bernie left the place a few months later, but on hot nights like tonight, Lucas can still catch the smell.

The first people arrive at six thirty; as soon as the doorbell rings, Lucas knows they can't be close friends of Manuel's, because most of his friends haven't even woken up yet. They talk about politics, about their jobs. Lucas can tell they're afraid of the neighborhood, will call a car service and be out of there before it gets dark. The doorbell rings again at six forty-five and to Lucas's surprise it's Diane. Even more surprising, she does not seem to know what to say to him. He mistakes it for sobriety, the awkwardness of being among the first people to arrive, while Diane wonders if all men have been wired to be so dense.

By eight o'clock, the party is moving, seventy-two pairs of feet cross the scratches and stains on that old floor. All of Diane's boyfriends are there: the fighter pilot Masoud is putting moves on Liz, who he knows is a lesbian but is smitten with anyway, and Liz humors him because he has eyes that remind her of her brother's, deep and lucid, before the schizophrenia began. Liz's roommates Izzy and The Slug are over by the window. Izzy is trying to see how many gallons of pudding fit in The Slug's pants; they're up to sixteen and the pants are just getting started. Erma and her lover Lucinda are eating the pudding that trickles out the leg; they feed each other with the blackened spoons they stole from the pocket of Robert Lord Townsend, Jr., a slumming junkie son of aristocracy who is too far gone to notice the theft, well, too far gone and transfixed by Ma Xiao Ling, a recent refugee who swam across the boat-torn Yangtze in a storm of slanting bullets and came to America in a crate full of sparking metal Godzilla and UFO toys. Ma Xiao Ling's two husbands, one for love and one for citizenship, are kickboxing in the far corner, their noses blowing a mist of blood; this match is refereed by the almost blind William McKay, a man in a wide wool cape who travels by hooking his cane to passing vehicles, then billowing out his cloak so that he is borne aloft, a sailor of the street. He was taught this trick by Isaac, who abandoned physics for the creation of robotic limbs; he is awaiting the patent that will make him wealthy enough to move to Greenland, where he will attempt to change his sleep cycle to match the daylight hours, passing most of the summer awake and most of the winter in slumber. He believes such a regimen will induce visions, an idea planted by Sylvia, the medium, whose tool for channeling spirits, a kickball, is being bounced around the room by Diane's four other boyfriends, the team of Ecuadorians, who form a human pyramid, then stand on the ceiling, then somersault in the air, ignoring gravity.

The Pan-Galactic Groove Squad crashes through the window at eleven thirty to claps and cheers and stomping feet; there are twenty-seven of them in this band, they have guitars and basses, keyboards, accordions, horns, banjos, and drums, so many drums, and they set up in no time and begin to play, a beat that starts down low and simple, just the kick and some hi-hat with one bass snaking around it. The rest of the band waits, they're letting the groove get in the pocket, hit bottom. It does; and now two drummers join in, they weave a polyrhythm that brings in one guitar and some pops from a banjo, oh this groove is young but it's growing, and people are starting to move. Now a singer steps up to the mike, puts out some blues that two more singers turn to gospel, harmonies deep and wide that make you want to believe. Five more drummers slip their way into the spaces, two guitars, another bass, a single trumpet line, simple and urgent, and those singers are swelling up, they're filling the groove to bursting, and just when nobody can take another second, they break it open in an explosion of horns and keyboards and shouting strings. The people open up their throats and sing, and everybody screams and throws their hands in the air, they're falling in and stomping it down, sweating and throwing back their heads until they are bound together, band and dancers, into a single thing, and this is a party not even the Hand of the Righteous could stop, it is loud and large and full of joy; and then Wendell steps into the room.

It is the entrance of the widow, frail and shaking, exhausted by grief. The band skids into silence, and for a moment, nobody wants to speak, nobody wants to poke a hole in the reverent air. They all look at him with uneasy smiles, and he looks back at them; and then Lucas hugs him, the condolences roll through the air, they raise glasses to him, to Manuel, to everyone, that they could be here tonight, and the band begins again, dropping a wicked swing, and everyone is moving again, grinning and kissing and yelling in each other's ears, inviting Wendell to start forgetting. Put him out of your head, they say. Join us and be happy.

But Masoud is not part of this, for something in Wendell takes him back to Lebanon. He thinks of his brother, angry and lost, a black marketeer for the mayhem and the intense profits involved, and because their father was gone. You are good with a gun, his brother said to him. I have seen what you can do. The crazy days in Beirut, sprinting down the street with bags of opium tied around his waist, vaulting over the traces of bullets, firing a round of ammunition into darkness out of a rifle that stamped bruises into his shoulder. Protect me, his brother said. But Masoud did not. Two years later, the same offer: protect me, now fringed with desperation; he had too many enemies, could not watch them all at once. Again Masoud did not help him, and left the country in grief and shame. He dealt in furniture supplies, stayed away from the business contracted behind the store. I will be a good man, he thought. There will be no more violence for me. But now here is Wendell, he does not ask but his face says it: protect me. And Masoud does not know what to do.

"I have a joke for you, Wendell," he says. "It is the funniest one I know. If you do not laugh, it is because you're not human."

"Masoud, I'm not—"

"—A man walks into a bar, and hears incredible music coming from the corner of the room. He looks around and, would a person look at that, there is an octopus sitting at a piano, playing like, who is that guy, Glenn Gould. That octopus is an amazing pianist, he tells the bartender. That's nothing, the bartender says. This octopus can play any instrument you give him."

Masoud suppresses a chuckle, the punch line is already starting to affect him. "So they give the octopus a clarinet and it plays it like, who? Benny, Benny Goodman. They give him an oud, do you know the oud? They give him an oud, and he plays it like . . . oh, you don't know the famous players. They give him a *triangle*—"

"—I get the idea."

"Okay, okay. So at last they give the octopus some bagpipes. And the octopus starts to wrestle with it, and the worst noise you have ever heard, he is making. Just terrible. The bartender and the man look at the octopus. I thought you said you could play any instrument you wanted, the bartender says. And the octopus says, *play* it? As soon as I get these pajamas off, I'm going to—"

The Groove Squad's horn section obliterates the last words. Masoud winces.

"I have to start over now, I think."

"Don't."

". . ."

". . ."

"I am sorry Manuel is gone."

"Thank you."

"No, I am serious. If you need anything . . ."

The Groove Squad blasts again, and the two are separated by a dervishing crowd of dancers rippling across Lucas's apartment. Wendell is spun in a horde of friendly hands, they are waiting for him to smile, but instead he turns his face to the ceiling, closes his eyes; and in the black vortex that follows, he thinks, as he has not since he met Manuel, of his father, though his death was years ago.

People start leaving the party at five in the morning, as dawn turns the city from blue to pink. The Pan-Galactic Groove Squad plays its last, the people in the band thank Lucas for having them and exit out the window. Those who remain end up on the roof, watching the sun pull itself out of the water and send heat sweeping across the island. They all grow quiet. It has been seventy-two hours since Manuel left them, seventy-two hours and there is still no sign. There is no scent in the rising steam, no notice in the papers. Nobody is calling to say they've found him. No messages appear in the harbor's water. In all the windows of the tenements and projects and luxury apartments suspended over the rivers, in the delis and sweatshops and butchers in Queens with skinned goats strung up in the window, the taquerías rank with sausage and cheese and chattering with telenovelas, the magazine stores and bodegas, there is nothing of him left. They kiss each other's foreheads, they wrap each other tight, and even though the sky is getting brighter and brighter, they all feel like saying good night. The Witnesses of the Ascension of González are trying to make their peace, to settle their crawling rage; but in Wendell it will not settle, it rattles and claws at his brain until the words come: I will go and find him.

CHAPTER 2

In Which Wendell Gets
Blood on His Shirt

 Nobody Owns a Purple Bathing Suit

On the highway across Broad Channel, out to the Rockaways,
between the Italian neighborhoods and the closed communi-
ties that line the beaches, there is a place where the land becomes skinny, the soil dissolves into marsh, and the city gives
way to weather-battered buildings and tackle shops, slanting
wooden houses with windsocks nailed to the back that look
over the broad expanse of Jamaica Bay: flat water spotted with
clumps of grass, laced with the wakes of motorboats, the sky
above broken by the planes landing at Kennedy. Far away,

beyond the water, the skyscrapers of Manhattan spike above the land, silver and gray, unreal.

Swami Horowitz's house was dragged into Jamaica Bay by a storm in 1954 that put half the neighborhood underwater. He was in his bedroom when it happened, under the covers with an issue of *Weird Tales* that his mother wouldn't let him read, stuff rots your mind, she used to say. He remembers that night as a few hours when something was revealed to him, in the way the house lifted off its foundation with a long groan and became buoyant, then was carried offshore, rocking from side to side, so that marbles and baseballs rolled from one side of the room to the other, while the first floor filled with water and he could hear his parents scratching at the ceiling below.

He swam back to shore after the storm passed, an orphan at fifteen. Relatives in Iowa and Montana offered to take him in, raise him as their own; the captain of a tugboat near Hell Gate offered to drag the house back to shore free of charge, a contractor would put it back on its foundation for a pittance. Swami Horowitz rejected all offers. He used a small part of his inheritance to build a pontoon bridge from his neighbor's dock to the second floor of the house, forty-two yards out in the water, installed a woodstove in his parents' bedroom. He worked at the marina, used the bathroom there, took showers. Come back to the land, they said. Come where it is dry and secure. But he'd been reading about plate tectonics, and he remembered how the house was once still, and how it had moved. What it had done.

"I will not be caught off guard again," Swami Horowitz said. "One day the land will move as the water does. One day this city will suffer another catastrophe. When that happens, I will be prepared."

Wendell has come to see Swami Horowitz because Swami Horowitz knows everyone. He has a gigantic diagram on the ceiling of his parents' bedroom that shows how everyone is related to everyone else. Names on slips of paper, fixed to the ceiling with long nails. Threads connect the names, black for relatives, green for friends, red for lovers, yellow for enemies. Purple for acquaintances: all relationships outside of blood tend to drift toward this, Swami Horowitz says. Wendell finds his name above the nightstand, and yes, green threads run to Lucas, to Diane, to half the members of the Pan-Galactic Groove Squad. A black thread running halfway across the ceiling connects to his cousin Reginald, an electrician in the Bronx whom Wendell hasn't seen in three years. And a red line shoots to Manuel above the foot of the bed. Manuel's nail is thick with thread, rays of color burst away from it, shocks streaking across the room. Other red threads that make Wendell wince.

"You knew, didn't you?" Swami Horowitz says.

" . . . "

"People who see this thing, it always upsets them a little. Always something in it they thought they wanted to know."

"Swami, do you have any idea where he is?"

"No. I haven't seen him in weeks, only heard about him. And the parties. They must have been tremendous."

"They were."

"I'm sorry I didn't see them—"

"—Swami . . ."

"Yes."

"I'm trying to find him. If you don't know where he is, you must know someone who does."

"You're serious."

"Yes."

"The police have already questioned all his friends. No-body knows."

"I know."

Swami ascends a stepladder, strums the threads on Manuel's nail, sings New York, New York, it's a hell of a town, the Bronx is up and the Battery's down . . .

"No one's talked to his enemies yet," he says. "The police don't know who they are. Try this man." He points to a name connected by a thick yellow line: Arturo "El Flaco" Domínguez. "A Dominican immigrant. He lives up in Washington Heights, but you won't find his name on the buzzer. You'll have to ask around, tell them who you are and what you're looking for."

"But if he hates Manuel—"

"—Don't worry." Swami Horowitz says. "He doesn't have anything against you. Coffee?"

"No . . . no, I should go."

"Wendell. Have some coffee."

They sip Maxwell House with their legs out the window of Swami Horowitz's sister's room, facing the expanse of the bay. The long spit of sand of Breezy Point arcs to their left, and be-yond, the deep blue of the Atlantic, waves pulsing in from hundreds of miles out, cut through by tankers and freighters, busier at the mouth of the bay, then quieter and quieter, until at last there is only the rippled expanse of open ocean, water heaving and falling as it did when the dinosaurs died, as it will when we are replaced by insects.

"I think I know why you want to find him," Swami Horowitz says. He swings his legs back into the house and beckons with a finger. Wendell finds him in his parents' bedroom on the stepladder with a hammer. He is wiggling Manuel's nail loose; he starts to pull it out and a web of strings strains after it, they pull tight, tighter, other nails begin to ache to the side. Strings go slack, threaten to fall off, others are sure to break. The whole system weakens.

"I designed it this way, you see. If Manuel is really gone, his departure will strain friendships, destroy others. Some lovers may part. And all those acquaintances, all the people who are just becoming friends, who are just beginning to exchange phone numbers, meet for meals on weekdays, swap books, slip notes and photos under each other's doors, learn about the sticky stuff that stayed on your hand for three days when you were five, share the good drugs they've been keeping for special occasions, talk about comic books starring people from Jupiter, have dinner on weekends, sleep together, move to the Gulf Coast and have beautiful children . . . all those people who are so close to this, their toes right on the edge, those chances will be taken away from them, just like that. It's a terrible thing when someone goes."

He sees Wendell off across the floating bridge, and after Wendell is out of sight, Swami Horowitz returns to his parents' room to fix the nail, to pull the threads tight again; for he's not gone yet, no, maybe not yet. He goes to the drawer and pulls out his father's purple bathing suit and a tennis hat his mother wore, puts them down on the bed, and stares at them for hours.

Eleven years later, when he is at sea, Swami Horowitz will go naked, keep his clothes folded inside so he doesn't wear them out, slather himself in fish oil so he doesn't burn. He'll dose water with iodine, learn to cook fish bones into a thin soup that he can eat when all the meat is gone. He will marvel that always, just as his propane is running low and he considers throwing himself into the ocean, another ship will come. Sometimes two men, a man and woman, worse off than he is and begging for hooks and bait, sometimes a derelict with dried corpses on the deck; he will take what he can from below. But sometimes it will be a tanker packed with a small town's worth of people who will invite him aboard for thick stew, jambalaya, vegetables they grow in hydroponic tanks in the hold. Then there will be parties, jangling dance music from homemade metal instruments. They will have heard of him, and he them; he will recognize the emblem of the Free State of Oceanica tattooed on the captain's forehead. When Swami Horowitz pushes off from them at last, he will think about how the links break, but always re-form. His friends are far from him, and some are gone, but they carry each other across the world.

He Even Smells Like a Gringo

The Mexican pastries in the deli on the corner of 163rd and Broadway are four months old; Rubén, the owner, lets them fester there to remind his customers that they are not Mexican, they are Dominican, the people who survived the crack wars in the eighties, who saw their cousins and brothers go down in boxes or the backs of police cars years ago, and who are still here today, with bullets lodged in their limbs and kids in school. When the police come in, Rubén pumps the merengue loud to cover the sound of the goats and chickens being slaughtered by the Santeríans in the apartment upstairs. They kill them during the day and dance, they kill them at night, and, in the summer, when all the windows are open and you're basting in your own sweat, you can hear the cries of the animals and the music rising around them, joining in the air with the cumbias and reggae, the shouts from rooftops, the calls from fire escapes, words of hate, words of love. There were times in the eighties when the street was like World War One, two rows of men eviscerating each other with machine guns, and Rubén lay in his bed listening to the bullets bury themselves in the brick walls around him; in those times, he would convince himself that he would go back, tell his friends back in Santo Domingo about the Big Lie, life, liberty, and hiding from the law. Stay here; it's safer, it's cleaner. But on these summer nights, he remembers why he stays.

Rubén can see Wendell coming from four blocks away, white skin, glasses glinting, his clothes in colors nobody in this neighborhood wears. He is asking people things, a man waiting to use a pay phone, another about to wash his car, a woman selling bundles of socks. They all cock an ear, they're not used to his unrolled *r*'s, he must sound Texan to them, but in time they comprehend and point up Broadway. As he nears, their fingers focus on the glass door of Rubén's deli, foggy with scratches and the ghosts of bumper stickers. Of course Rubén knows what this is about; he just didn't think someone would come so soon.

"Are you looking for something?" Rubén says.

"My name is Wendell and I'm looking for El Flaco—"

In less than a second, Rubén has a gun out and he's sent a bullet by Wendell's ear. Wendell yelps and hits the floor, one hand over his head, yelling *jesus fuck,* his legs scrambling to propel his body toward the door, but Rubén already has the gun put away, and he's laughing.

"*Bueno, hombre.* I needed to know for sure that you were no cop." He extends his hand. Wendell refuses it.

"I'm ah . . . I'm looking for El Flaco. Arturo Domínguez, El . . ."

"Why do you need to see him?"

"It's about Manuel."

Rubén's eyebrows rise. He opens the cash register, puts the gun in the drawer, retrieves a note and reads it, reads it again. The television broadcasts a report of objects hovering over Queens. A nervous FAA official is interviewed at La Guardia. Could be balloons or military aircraft, he says, reading from an index card. Or mob-related. Everyone has helicopters these days.

"Wendell . . . Apogee?"

"Yes."

"I will take you to El Flaco. But first you must eat this." He lifts up the tray of Mexican pastries, revealing a plastic bag of lavender pills.

"I'm not taking one of those."

"You want to see El Flaco or no? I refuse to take you to him when you are conscious."

Wendell turns the pill over in his hand. In the first days after he fell in love, Manuel took him to a party on the roof of a building in the Financial District, a tall column of metal and glass shunted among office buildings that rose from the impossible depths below and curved into the air around them. The party hosts bribed the security guards, disabled the alarm systems, assumed control of the elevators, thinking they'd be able to maintain secrecy. This was a naïve fantasy. Too many people showed up, the music was too loud. The accountants and brokers working late that Saturday stared at them from adjacent office buildings, and Wendell thought for sure that they'd call the police when the partiers started getting naked and setting off fireworks. They did: an hour later, at about three thirty in the morning, the door to the stairwell was knocked off its hinges and a squad of private security guards with heavy ordnance scrambled onto the roof, ordering the partiers to cease and desist. The hosts were ready for this: the music stopped, the last fireworks bloomed in the air, and bedsheets were distributed to the guests, who began flinging themselves off the roof, unfurling the sheets above them to slow the forty-story fall to the street. The sheets spread out behind them, but they seemed to wriggle as if ready to collapse, and soon sheet and nudist were lost in the dark below; there was only the sound of their shouts, of glee or terror.

"Jump," Manuel said.

"No way," Wendell said.

"Do you want to go to jail?" He smiled and kissed him, then took a running leap off the edge, hollering like a cowboy. Wendell remembers, then, his own last strides across the rubberized roof, the vault over the railing, and then a slow, crazy spin over the street far below, fumbling with the sheet, the lights from offices marking the way down, the hoots of the others descending through the acrid dust that the fireworks left behind, and him thinking *Christ, how did Manuel get me into this, get me into so much trouble—*

He pops the pill into his mouth, and Rubén moves behind him to catch him when he falls.

Mr. Zero

The bulletin board behind Inspector Salmon's desk is too empty. On it is a photograph of Manuel with a sly smile on his face and what looks like a beer bottle in his hand. There are photographs of his most informative friends, a chronology of his last day in the city and the places he went; today, Salmon can add that he was last seen on the pier in Coney Island, for, by happy accident, one of his former lovers saw him there, said that Manuel was acting "strange . . . well, lucid and glad, which for him was strange." Salmon clings to this information, for it is the only thing he has learned since he finished interviewing Manuel's friends. He knows lots of stories now, but almost nothing about the man. Where he was from, since his birth certificate turned out to be fake. What he did for a living. How he came to know sixteen languages. How old he was.

"A nullity," Trout says. "The banks called today. They do not hold, nor have they ever held, accounts under any combination of his four names. No suspicious accounts have been closed of late. None have opened. There is more. Manuel Rodrigo de Guzmán González appears in exactly zero of our government agencies' records. Immigration and the IRS have nothing. Likewise the FBI, various state and local law enforcement agencies, Social Security, Medicare, Medicaid. You realize that he had only lived in his apartment for three weeks before it exploded and we do not know where he lived before that. Nobody does. Indeed, had his apartment not exploded, and had those celebrations in his honor not been visited by law enforcement, we might never have known that Mr. González existed in the first place. We are not tracking a ghost, or a man who disappeared. We are trying to find a man who was never here."

"But he *was* here."

"Really? Where is your evidence of that? You will say you have that photograph on the board. You only believe that is Mr. González because somebody told you it was. You will show me the volumes of testimony from his acquaintances, whom we interviewed. But this could be an artfully plotted scheme by a large group of people to divert us from a larger case. All these festivities could have been for some other reason. You know that for all our powers of investigation, detection, and analysis, there are many things that still elude us. We, the authorities, are aboard a raft floating on the surface of an opaque society. We may on occasion be able to reach into those obscure waters, see some movement down there, but so much happens in the depths. The bottom teems with a million species as yet undiscovered. Great beasts fight each other to the death. Cities of coral rise and fall, rise and fall. But we see none of this, save a stirring on the surface, a ripple sent up from the floor. Inspector Salmon: it is possible that something gigantic is being planned down there, maybe just out of sight, while we have been set up to chase a fiction."

"People don't fall in love with fictions."

"Don't they?"

"Don't start hypothesizing, deducing this much already, it's—"

"—This is not like the Lucy Rutman case at all, Salmon, and to be frank, I would appreciate your not bringing it up."

"You brought it up."

"You were going to."

"That case was years ago."

"Yes. Four years ago and yesterday."

"It's not the same thing."

"I am almost certain it's not, Salmon. But for the sake of this case, I know that, to balance an inevitable bias on your part, I must remain open and dispassionate. Even more dispassionate than I am accustomed."

". . ."

"Come now, Salmon, I mean you no harm. It is not your fault that you still have a heart."

"Manuel is real."

"I am almost certain that he is." He lays a hand on Salmon's shoulder. "Or at least was."

 Lavinia

". . . up. Wake up."

The heat is behaving like a liquid, it presses down on him, pours into his nose and mouth, blocks breathing. Wendell is strapped to a Barcalounger that does not hurt him but will not let him go. It is reclined, and points his head at a ceiling writhing with steam and water pipes, hissing and dripping. I am in a basement, he thinks; but no, beyond his feet, across the half-rotten parquet floor, the outline of light from a window, blocked by heavy black curtains. An electric stove is rusting in the corner; now and again it sparks and jumps, and the fan overhead wobbles. El Flaco, dressed in a brown wool suit, is sitting in a wooden chair, legs crossed, arms folded across his torso, a lit cigarette in one hand, cup of hot coffee in the other.

"Please do not take the restraints as a sign that I do not trust you. How do you know I exist?"

He takes a mouthful of coffee, swishes it in his mouth, spits it onto the floor. Now the cigarette is between his lips. He breathes in, waits. Wendell says nothing. El Flaco blows smoke.

"The police have heard of me but do not know I am real. Los Mariachis del Fuego, who say they know you, have promised they would say nothing. Manuel is gone now, and anyway told you nothing for years."

"What are you involved in? Drugs?"

"A forward question. But I see the game you are playing so I will answer it. No, I am not involved in drugs. That is a degenerate trade. I am involved in the trade of people. Parts of people sometimes—such a look you give me. They are dead already."

"How's business?"

"How's business, he asks. Like two floor managers at Sears, talking to each other in the food court. How's business. Mr. Apogee, business is, how do you say it, business is booming. You have no idea how many people go in and out of this country every day. Every day, thousands of them. Oh, Homeland Security gets a few, but I get many of the rest. Boats, trains. A few planes. There are people that come in tied to the bottoms of pickup trucks. Sewn into couches. Some of the Homeland Security people, they are illegals I put there, though of course Homeland Security does not know this, they think they are from Dayton. Heh. From Dayton, Ohio, speaking Colombian Spanish. Though you think they know that . . . ?"

"Sounds like you know what you're doing."

"Do not act like you are friends with me."

"I'm just trying to be friendly."

"So cocky you talk, as if you are not scared, what is the word, shitless? Do not play with me, I know the kind of man you are. You are a man who on an ordinary day would never come to this neighborhood, who, if he finds himself here, leaves as fast as he can. Who does not speak a single word of Spanish, who does not see in the cut of his clothes the marks of disposable income, who believes himself a target all because he has skin the color of a dead fish. Do not flatter yourself. The people in this neighborhood, they do not care if you are here or not. If I were to cut your throat, take out your windpipe and shove it in your mouth, then throw the body out the window, they would all turn their eyes from you and walk away. They were here in the eighties. They have seen your kind before. That you know nothing of this shows how Manuel deceived you."

"And you too, it seems."

"Does your fear make you rave, or are you an idiot? There is little that Manuel hid from me that I did not discover. His plans for me would have put me in prison, capital offenses, but he did not realize how much I could pay them, what information I had about their past."

"He was trying to destroy your business?"

"Business? You know nothing of any of this, do you? I thought you knew him. They all said you knew him, that he told you everything."

"What did he do?"

"He stole my wife. Lavinia. The woman who saved my life in the mountains of Peru when a bandit had his machine gun in my ear. The woman who was with me on the long run to Japan, when we, what is it, smuggled people into the port at Kobe. She was with me for the big run into San Francisco, four hundred and twenty-four Chinese, the papers I made said they were a marching band, coming to America to buy instruments and prosthetic limbs for war veterans, a joke so ludicrous that Homeland Security—ah, though it was the INS then—had no choice but to believe. That was the job that made me the man I am today, and she was there for that. I know we used to dream together the same things, we used to ask each other in the morning, and they were always the same. But he discovered how to take her away. He must have used drugs and magic. He knew I would come for him when I discovered what he did, so he, he conspiracied to put me in prison. I rose above that, but my Lavinia is gone away with him. This is why I hate him, the man who was my best *coyote,* the man I trusted most. This is why I want to find him. He did not destroy my business and he did not kill me. No: he took the one thing from me that I would not have gladly given him and left me alive after it. For this I wish to see him dead."

He drags on the cigarette, screws it against the side of the stove, then drinks the rest of the coffee, long and slow. Then he unfolds his legs and rises, and now Wendell understands the nickname, for El Flaco is a stretched man, the fan tickles his scalp and his shirt hangs off his collarbones, falls straight to the hem, his knees jut from his pants like spurs, and his face and hands, they are all bone and tight skin, clenched tendons, eyes rolling in strung flesh.

"But now I have told you many things," he says. "I have done this in the spirit of the game I believe you are playing. I have done this in the hope that you will tell me now the one thing I want to know. For I have looked for the answer in all the neighborhoods. I have gone to Darktown and asked in the bars and in the market, and they—"

"Darktown? What's Dark—?"

"—Do not interrupt me. I have gone there and asked, and bought many rounds, and they still cannot tell me: where is Manuel?"

"Where . . ."

"Yes. Where is he?"

"I . . . I came here to ask you that."

For four seconds, El Flaco does not move. Then he cocks his head to one side, as if figuring out a puzzle.

"They said you would know, Mr. Apogee. They said there was nothing he did not tell you, that you were the one he loved. More than my Lavinia."

"I don't know where he is. I came here looking for him myself."

"Then you must go." He claps twice, and behind the door to the room, there is shuffling, someone banging something against the wall. "Before we put you down again, let me warn you: I believe you will not find González. I believe the search for him will kill you. Turn back from this. Move out of this city, go to the West Coast, where people find peace and do not remember what happened three days ago . . . ah, but I see you cannot do that."

A man named Tomás enters the room, his oversize forearms carrying a large two-by-four.

"Our supply of pills runs low. Turn your head away from the blow, and Tomás will ensure that you suffer no, what is it, permanent damage. You may feel nothing at all."

Wendell turns his head, and it is as El Flaco said: there is a grunt from Tomás, a whistle in the air. Perhaps the instant the wood touches the back of his head, there is a slight pressure, the buzz of displaced electrons; perhaps not.

 **$576**

Shouts, whistles, rising hollers, the flurry of batting feathers, and then cheers, chattering voices, the slip of money changing hands. For a minute, Wendell can see nothing, thinks Tomás blinded him, but then he realizes it's because his shirt is tied around his face. Claws scrabble on concrete. Squawks. The voices rise, they are shouting at each other, another blitz of wings cuts through a commotion of limbs.

He is in the corner of a brown basement lit by yellowed fluorescent bulbs, strewn with dried flowers, plastered with cracked posters of Mexican musicians. Los Tigres del Norte bounce from a radio somewhere, polka drums and tight harmonies, the blare of an accordion. The place is packed with men, a few women, children with plastic bags of peanuts poke through the crowd, a man pushes a cooler full of beers on a luggage cart, calling *cerveza helada, cerveza helada,* his voice buried in the roaring cheers.

In the middle of the room, in a tight circle, two cocks are tearing into each other with razored spurs tied to their feet, the floor under them slick with the blood of previous matches, mangled feathers, pieces of flesh, here and there an occasional eye, a broken beak. One of them collapses and the crowd cheers;

their handlers are on them, they put the bloody heads in their mouths to revive them, then release them again. The birds dance around each other for a few seconds; then in a storm of feathers and flapping they carve muscles out of each other, pull apart, come together again. Within a minute one of the cocks is staggering away, shiny with blood; the neck turns at an odd angle, the animal flops over into its own gore, and the crowd rises and hollers, money is thrown around in a rage of coins and paper.

The owners of the cocks enter the ring. One picks up his bird by the legs and carries it out swinging, mutters to himself when a spat of blood lands on his shoe. He bought the bird in Tennessee, had it shipped to El Salvador to be trained and then smuggled back to the United States, going through five middlemen to distance himself from the proceedings. This business with the cocks, his wife said, it's unseemly. Why can't you satisfy yourself with real estate or venture capital? He could not answer, did not know; it was the risk, maybe, the investment in the bird, the danger of associating yourself with men who killed animals for sport. He liked it. But not tonight: this bird was expensive, well-bred, well-fed, trained hard. It had killed two birds already, but those were little matches, not enough to make back the money he'd put in. He is still two thousand short, and now the bird is dead, and he has blood on his shoe. The start of a bad night.

Three more of his birds wait near the door in shiny cages. "Don't screw me," he says to them, and throws the corpse at a trainer who, he thinks with disgust, may try to eat it.

The other owner gathers his bird in both arms, holds it to his chest, strokes its head, lets the blood soak into his shirt.

It was his only bird, found skulking along the road outside Chimaltenango; he was going to kill it and cook it until he watched it blind a cat that tried to prey on it. My lucky bird, he thought. Two fights later and he had enough to pay Manuel Rodrigo de Guzmán González to ship them both to Brooklyn in a Saudi freighter, the bird sedated in a crate marked as high-end citrus, he passing as Aziz, on shore leave from the merchant marine. He believed in his bird too much, put everything he had on it; now it is gone, and as the blood seeps to his skin he understands with an awful simplicity that he is stranded alone in this alien place, and does not know what he is going to do. He stands there, cradling the carcass in red-slicked arms, and watches as another eager man pulls a fresh cock from the chicken-wire cage at the back of the stairs, pats the bird on the head, and ties knives to its feet.

"Wendell? . . ." It is Masoud, a wad of bills in his hand. "I did not know you came to these things. How much have you won? Today is a beautiful day for me, I have bet in six matches and won five."

"What time is it?"

"Pardon?"

"Time, what time is—?"

"—Ah, yes, yes. Three thirty."

". . . in the morning?"

"Of course in the morning, you can't hold something like this in the daytime, the neighbors complain about the smell. How much have you won?"

"I . . . haven't bet yet."

"You have a few more minutes to bid on this one. The second bird doesn't have the razors on yet . . . Are you all right?"

"Yes."

Masoud peers at him. "I did not see you come in."

His brother's office in Beirut: a desk in a cinder block alleyway behind a store that sold radios and microphones. His brother is sitting at it in a tan suit with an infected gash over his eye. Brother, I need you. They'll kill me if they catch me.

Masoud stares. I am a pacifist now. I have killed too many people already. In the war. Hundreds.

His brother stares back. If you do not protect me, I will die.

Then the boat heaves in the uncommon chop of the Mediterranean, bearing him away from the shore of his country. He wonders if any of his ancestors had helped make the alphabet, make the dead speak, make others remember things that they did not live. He grips the rail, holds his stomach. Seasickness. Had I protected him. Had I stayed. The million tendrils streaming from his life into fiction, the things he did not do.

"You are looking for Manuel," he says.

" . . ."

"It used to be that he was always here. He made bets for fantastic sums of money, tens of thousands of dollars on the head of a bird. I do not know which one made him happier, winning or losing." They are shouldered apart for a minute by a man bearing the body of a gutted cock, beak chipped, entrails loose and hanging.

"I thought you were a pacifist."

"I am. But I make an exception for cockfights. Nostalgia, you see. It reminds me of when I was young with my cousins and brother and my father. Those were days, heh, those were days when if you told me that I was going to be a fighter pilot, fighter pilot then pacifist, I would have laughed. Laughed and then beaten you with a wooden board. But those days are long behind me now. It is better to be as you must have been, Wendell. Studious. A smart kid who used his head. Settled."

"Maybe," Wendell says. They watch the next match, where a small greenish bird hops into the air and slices open a large brown bird from below the beak to between the legs; the body peels open and viscera bloom from it, the animal slumps forward and rests on the pile to the shocked shout of its owner and the rapturous cheers of the ones who bet on the underdog.

"Do eh . . . can you understand this? One morning after the fights, Manuel took me to a diner and asked me if I wanted to fly a . . . I am not sure what he was talking about, some kind of machine. I told him I only had experience with Russian planes, the MiGs and nothing else. He waved his hands at me. He'd seen papers about me, and he was sure I could do it. Do what, I asked. So he grabbed the hair on the back of my head and pushed me in close. You have the skill to do it, he said, but I can't tell you what it is unless you agree to be saved. Saved, he said. I did not know he was religious."

"He wasn't. Isn't. He once got a Jew for Jesus drunk just to steal his T-shirt."

"Then what did he mean?"

"I don't know."

"I do not know what he was talking about either, but it sounded . . . big."

"How long ago was this?"

"Four months ago. Five, maybe."

"Saved from what—?"

Upstairs, glass breaks, someone screams, it's the police raiding the building on account of the smell of chicken blood on the street that not even four incense vendors stationed outside could cover. Stop, freeze, hold it right there, the officers yell, put your hands in the air, but they're not even down the stairs. The fight ringleaders run to the back of the room shouting *mira, mira,* they fumble with panels in the wall that slide aside and reveal steps leading down, under the basement, under the neighboring building, smelling of rat piss and stale cockroaches, but it's that or the cops, so everyone hustles down, pushing and shoving, until the room is emptied and the panels slide back, hiding all. When the police storm the basement, they find only walls, posters, bottles, empty bags of potato chips, disemboweled chickens lying in the ring.

In the dark chaos, Wendell has lost Masoud again; the people on the steps above and below are strangers to him, speaking a language he does not understand. It was like this at his father's death, him in his room at night, upright in the bed with the door open to the hall, as the policeman explained the condition of the body to his mother, who stood there with a handkerchief over her mouth. Wendell's father: spendthrift, would-be entrepreneur, too enamored of science fiction movies in which people in silver suits glide across cities, arms at sides in vacuum tubes. He constructed a network of them around the house, glass on the straightaways, plastic on the turns, curving out of windows and circling over the roof to plunge into the back door, until the house looked like a frozen octopus.

The tubes ended in the basement, at the vacuum-producing behemoth his father called Terminus A. He did calculations, he made adjustments to the angle of the tubing; he sent grapefruits, watermelons through the system, then a side of frozen beef. All seemed in order.

"He did not realize," said the policeman, "that it wasn't his weight that mattered, it was his length. He equipped Terminus A with such a powerful vacuum that, beginning at the turn that enters your kitchen window out there, the pull on your husband's head was so much greater than the pull on his feet that . . . well." He did not want to mention it, but the glass and plastic were clear if you wanted to see the long slick of tissue, blood, and bone, the shreds of his silver suit, which he had stitched together at the sewing machine not a week before, giggling and giddy.

"There is something heroic in it," the policeman continued. "One day, when our spacefaring descendants lose control of their craft and fall into black holes, if they survive the friction, the intense heat, they will go the same way, as they approach the singularity, the heart of what could have been a supernova."

Wendell's mother refused to recover. She withdrew from friends, shrank from the men who courted her: Mr. Stevenson, the balding owner of a small chain of Laundromats, and Mr. Eckerd, a hockey coach, both good men. For a time, Wendell followed her, parts of him becoming older than was fair. Wrinkles in his head. But then he made a decision: I will not die young. I will take this thing and be stronger. He boarded a bus, his $576 inheritance folded in his shirt pocket, fists clenched and angry, ready to tear down buildings; but even this passed.

"I want things to be quiet," he'd once said to Manuel, and Manuel laughed.

"You love me too much for that," he said.

Below him, the stairs turn to wood and light flows between the slats. Other people are moving below them, carrying bundles and laughing at each other; then the floor to his right opens out and reveals a bright cavern far below, swathed in inky yellow glow; there is music, voices, the sound of engines. Steel cables mounted around him descend into a nest of suspended houses, noise, people clambering on a web of ladders, and, far below, the grumble of invisible boats. Another city below this one, another place.

"What is it?" Wendell asks.

"*La ciudad . . .,*" the man behind him says. "The city . . . city of the dark? You go there?"

"No—no, I—"

"You . . . you should," says the man. "It is the place . . . *es el lugar donde se encuentran cosas perdidas,* the place where you find lost things. . . ."

Wendell wants to tell this to Masoud, to speak in a voice that will make Masoud know he has learned something important. But Masoud is not here. They are shuffling into the dark, hands out in front of them, feeling the walls, telling quiet jokes to each other. Punch lines that make those around him laugh, but he didn't hear the joke, doesn't know why they're funny. Sold her my thermos for sixty dollars. Hope you've got four. I've been in and out of puddles all day. Fuck 'em, they're bees.

Somebody help me. I can't do this myself.

It Meant Something Before Cassius Clay Was Even Born

They emerge at six thirty through a drainage pipe emptying into the Hudson. The river is orange with morning, the George Washington Bridge leaps over the river, cars shine across it, honking at each other. The people in front of Wendell look like survivors of a massacre, chicken blood strewn over their clothes; they pull their arms over their heads and blink, as if waking up. For a time, the group is gathered at the pipe's edge, contemplating the traffic on the Henry Hudson above, the few sailboats below, the greenery on the top of the Palisades that makes New Jersey seem so inviting sometimes, but before long, they are dispersing, going home. Many of them can see their apartments from there, they live right up in those broken-down buildings above the freight tracks, but for Wendell, it is a long way back to Astoria. He has never gotten used to this idea, that a few miles could take hours to cross, and as he switches from train to bus, crossing the span of the Triborough Bridge, he can feel the city expand beneath his feet, stretching over the curve of the planet, a buzzing network of manholes and mazed asphalt, canals, crouching brown-stones and leaning tenements, offices knifing into the sky, un-til it is easy to believe that all the world is like this, though of course it isn't. And there is the place below him, a place he's sure is everywhere now: when he gets off the bus at Steinway, he crouches and puts his ear to a sewer grate, is sure he catches strains of subterranean merengue.

The air conditioner in Egypt Café is broken, so the door is open, and Daoud is sitting at the first table drinking hibiscus tea and smoking sweet tobacco from a water pipe. When he opened the restaurant, he and his sister Zeineb threw Egypt on the walls: masks, pages from books, photographs of family members, Muhammad Ali, and colonials on camels, a set of pipes and a half of a dumbek, a rotting electric guitar, dried flowers, rusty paintings on wooden boards, seven thousand years and the sweep of invader after invader who banged new shapes into the people and left them when the money ran out. The people per-sisted. The history of Egypt is written in its food, Daoud is fond of saying. The Greeks and the Romans brought us olive oil, the Europeans brought us tomatoes and potatoes and beef. The great hopes of Muhammad Ali, the fever of the Mahdi and the defeats of Nasser are written in the sand in fava beans grown from the ashes of the library of Alexandria; all of this sustains us.

Daoud expels smoke as Wendell enters. "What's wrong with you. You look like you went to a cockfight."

"I did."

"Did you win or lose?"

"I didn't bet."

"Who goes to a cockfight and doesn't bet?"

"It wasn't my idea. I was dragged there."

Daoud laughs. "Ah, one of those kinds of nights. Yes. Come, come, sit back here with me, away from the door. I have things to tell you." He sets falafel to frying, puts on a John Lee Hooker tape, and then sits so that he throws a shadow across Wendell's face; there is a part of him that loves this.

"You should have seen the party in here. Crazy. Too crazy. Of course I love it."

"I did see it. The end of it, anyway."

"I can close for a month, take my family to Egypt to visit my mother, the money I made on that night."

"Are you going to?"

"No, no, they can go. I forgot how to be on vacation, I'm not any good at it anymore."

"What did you have to tell me?"

He leans in close. "I have heard you are looking for Manuel."

"I am . . . how did you know?"

"Masoud. He was here an hour ago. He looked worse than you did, like he'd been dragged by a bus. You know that Manuel came here to visit me the day before he left. In the afternoon. He had a cup of good coffee. We talked about Nusrat Fateh Ali Khan—have you heard this man sing?—and then he said something very strange. He told me he was leaving, and when I asked him where, he pointed at the ceiling—"

The pay phone on the wall rings, and Daoud stands to get it. "Talk to me, baby," he begins, and then rockets along in a mix of Arabic and Spanish with Italian inflections. He laughs, large and deep. Then a *ciao, baby,* and he hangs up, takes the falafel from the pan, arranges it on a plate with hummus and greens, dusts all with a touch of cumin, and hands it to Wendell.

"This is falafel, hummus . . . heh you know what it is, I say it so many times a day it is habit now. I am like a cooking parrot. Sit and eat . . ." He sits again. ". . . while I tell you this most important thing. Wendell, some people came in here, looking for you. I don't know who they were, but they were huge. They could not get through the door. All of them wearing giant purple raincoats. Where do you live, where do you work, they were asking these things, but even if I knew I would not have told them. Wendell, I know you are not involved in anything, you are a good man, but maybe it is like what Trotsky says, you may not be interested in trouble, but trouble is interested in you—well, he says that about Marxism but you get my point . . . why don't you stay here for the afternoon, I make you an early dinner?"

"Daoud, it—"

"—Stay. So I know you are safe."

The smoke smells of apples and warmth, it drifts into him, loosens his legs, his shoulders, and he and Daoud talk of neighborhood politics, how the Greeks are ceding land to the Arabs, how the Central Americans are making things interesting, fleeing wars and governments full of thieves, coming here to open restaurants and sell real estate. The neighborhood gets better all the time, Daoud says. It is evolution. There is talk of Daoud's family, of his upbringing in Egypt, the sun-blasted shores of the wide Nile and the moneychangers in Cairo. Sometimes they say nothing; they just sit there smiling and smoking and eating vegetables. Within two months, when he is huddled under a blanket in three inches of water, peering up through the bright grate of a rain gutter at the fury in the street above, the sparks from the great fires fluttering down through the dark air, scaring away the vermin, he will think back on this afternoon, the last quiet hours he had. He will want to travel back in time to tell himself to savor it, the taste of the food and tobacco in the hot shade, the sound of Daoud's jovial voice over the gritty, bouncy ragtime he is fond of; he will want to tell himself to draw it in and keep it, cup it in his shivering hands, curl around it, and allow it to bring him sleep, in the forty-five minutes between the flames and the sudden flight.

Angry Ghosts

It is 2:06 in the afternoon, and the sun burns through the windows, makes fires in the air of Diane's bedroom, it's baking the paint off the walls, it's melting the light fixtures into chrysalis shapes. Diane is in bed with the Ecuadorians; the four of them are snuggled around her, snoring in tandem, twitching sometimes. They all should be at work today, Diane at Strong Belief, Inc., a printing shop that specializes in pamphlets and flyers. *We Do Manifestoes*, their sign reads. They've printed fund-raising flyers for the New York representatives of the IRA and EZLN, men with slick suits and hints of accents who both refer to their employers as "my organization." They do booklets for various cloistered fanatics in the greater New York area; the majority live on Staten Island for some reason. These people see order in the dispersal of bottle caps on deli floors, they see something sinister in the pattern of trash cans and advertisements for municipal services. Diane's favorite is Erwin Gruenwald, a Forest Hills resident whose elegies for the slow death of the pay phone create in her an uneasy wonder. Gruenwald's work takes the form of epic poetry, obtuse, encyclopedic, and allegorical: the pay phone appears as a once-glorious fighter weakened by age, who has repelled the assaults of snow, animals, car crashes, and teenagers with power tools and crowbars, only to be vanquished by an enemy he cannot see: the cellular phone, which appears as a fog of whispering voices that implore the hero to commit suicide. Give up, they say. You cannot defeat us. Climb to the tallest tower and hurl yourself therefrom. Diane believes the work tells a vague truth about cell phones, how people who use them are like the living dead, victims of possession, or schizophrenics, walking down the street oblivious, staring at nothing, mumbling or shouting into their own hand. Previous eras would not have been kind, Gruenwald writes: sent to asylum, thrown in the lake; gelded or exiled, burned at the stake; in our age redeemed, for technology's sake. Gruenwald then mentions that he is a mere five generations removed from tree frogs. But Diane knows what he means: some days, the street is populated by mannequins and suits and construction gear, toting briefcases and cups of coffee, noticing nothing of what is happening around them. She wants to run from person to person, shake them by the shoulders, yell *wake up, wake up . . .*

Had the Ecuadorians not stayed with Diane, had they piled into their studio apartment in Long Island City that they share with eleven other people, they would be out at JFK by now, resurfacing runways while the planes hover in with a roar from Europe, shriek overhead on their way to Los Angeles, obliterating the radio in the truck tinning out hip-hop, the stuff that's still mining the funk mother lode from the seventies. Their job is dangerous: the runways are scarred with crosses, crescents, stars of David, food, and a burning lamp on a wooden table, the markings of the Angels of the Airport. The Ecuadorians have seen a man decapitated by landing gear as he attempted to run; they have heard stories of runway men incinerated in the engines of planes taking off, of men caught by the stomach on the edge of a wing and carried, across the Atlantic, across the Pacific, choking to death at 30,000 feet amid piled cumulus clouds, the curved continents splayed out below.

But none of them are in any of those places. It is 2:07 in the afternoon. Outside, stocky women in flowery dresses chat on orange plastic chairs in front of the Laundromat. Two boys fence with broom handles in the street, rap the fenders of cars when they pass by and run away laughing when the driver hits the brakes. The sun is keeping the Ecuadorians asleep; they dream back to the places they came from, it seemed like the weather was like this all the time, deep green and malarial, where there was no work, just houses made of scrap metal, but the birds were exquisite and the women fine, women who could throw you across the room. They shift in their sleep and draw closer, and Diane loves this about them, her boys, her little guys. They saved her one day, you see: a psychotic had attacked her on the Nevins Street train platform, pistol-whipping her and tugging down her pants, when the Ecuadorians flew down from the I-beams, jumped up from the tracks, out of the grout between the tiles on the wall, kicking and punching, until the criminal fled up the stairs and she opened her eyes to four hands reaching to help her up. She has been to their soccer games in the park, watched them fly like angry ghosts across the field, she has clapped and cheered for them, but now, even with them around her snoring in fugue, she can't help but think of Lucas. His apartment, a mere mile or two away down Van Brunt; his floor, scarred by bones and dancing feet; his arms, tattooed with the signs of the Lunar Temple, that in her daydreams are around her, are moving down her sides, down to her rising hips. She fell in love with him when he fixed her stove, lifting it off the floor with a car jack, then sliding underneath; again when he raided a furniture-making sweatshop on Fourth Avenue with the Hand of the Righteous; again when she was put down for a week by a violent flu and he visited her for hours every day, reading the Bhagavad Gita aloud until she fell asleep. That is Lucas to her, cold, just, and kind, and she vows to have him someday; but this thought makes her liver writhe in her abdomen, her pancreas try to turn inside out. Isn't it enough, her organs say, to be here in the sun with people who love you? It is, it is. But her heart says: it's not, it's not.

 Another Fire

It must be too hot to eat, for not a customer has come into Egypt Café. Daoud is red with wine, pounding the table with his big hands, voice booming; Wendell is slumped against the wall, riding off his seat in a fit of tearing laughter that makes him have to take off his glasses, wipe them on his shirt, again and again. The air mellows to orange, the office workers start to come back from Manhattan in blouses and ill-fitting suits, the tide of buses and Lincoln Town Cars ebbs and flows with every change of stoplight. Across the street, the Mexican kids who live in the building stop chasing cockroaches on the sidewalk and go into the Tycoon Deli for tacos and Jarritos pineapple soda. Now the first customers of the night come in, tentative, wondering how two people could make such a ruckus. The afternoon is closing; and Wendell tries to pay Daoud, but he waves it away, so Wendell spins outside and shuffles toward his apartment, hands in pockets to attempt stability.

He rounds the corner to his block and is within sight of his apartment when Masoud streaks down the block on his bicycle, jumps off, and tackles Wendell into the sparse shrubs under a white plastic statuette of St. Francis of Assisi. Wendell wants to complain, but Masoud has already pinned him down, he has his hand over his mouth.

"Be still! You must be still!" Masoud's voice flutters, he shakes with terror.

From Wendell's window come flashes of green and purple light, scuttles and shrieks. Then a howl that sets the dogs barking for blocks, cats fighting and mating in the alleys to ripping each other to pieces. A glow grows, phasing from blue to orange, and with a scream that breaks glass, the window frames shatter outward and four shapes in purple raincoats fly out, mounted on tiny hovering scooters that emanate a fine red mist. They wheel around each other and then shoot down the canyon of air between the buildings to lift off into the sky; seconds later, an explosion fires from the ruined wall, the flames leap across the street and warp the glass of the apartments on the other side. Wendell's apartment is then a smoking hole, gawked at by neighbors, the tatters of his possessions snowing into the street: the limbs of furniture, cushion fluff, and books, hundreds of books burning and flopping to the ground, trailing fire and ash. Someone must have called the fire department, because they can hear the trucks hollering closer, just a few blocks away; but a small crowd has already formed, they're talking to each other and pointing up at the side of the place, at the smoldering table hanging halfway out, legs snapped off and splintered, aching to fall.

"I . . . I saw them go in," Masoud says. "I was coming to see you, to make sure you got away from the fights, and I saw them in there. Wendell, who are they?"

"I don't know. Daoud said they were looking for me. . . ."

Wendell's home has settled in the street by now, dented pans and broken plates, the spines of novels, photographs of friends and family, scraps of shirts and pants, souvenirs from his meandering days after his father died, a packet of beef jerky from North Carolina, the punched-out and twisted remnants of a banjo he'd bought for twenty-five dollars but never learned to play. All is on the pavement now, or dressing parked cars, and the speculators pick at the debris, half-guilty, half-scared, as if the dead things still hold fire from the bomb that destroyed them, coiled energy that could leap out and explode again.

"The police will arrive soon," Masoud says. "The Inspectors again . . . I am sure someone told them."

"I don't want to see them," Wendell says.

"They will not suspect you of anything," Masoud says. "Not if you stay here. If you run, they may think many things. They may think you are part of all this, that you and Manuel are connected."

I am a part of this. We are connected. You are flying away from me, babe, you are sinking into dark water, and I am tethered by the ankle. I will follow you until the air runs out.

"You are going anyway," Masoud says.

"Yes."

His brother lying on the street in Beirut; the heaving ship. The things he did not do, the fictions that could have been his life.

"Then I am coming with you," Masoud says.

"Why?"

"Because this is part of something larger than us. Something big is going to happen, and I want to be ready when it does." He regards the ruins before him. "And besides," he says, "you are my friend." And thinks: brother, this time I will save you.

The buildings twist, their colors change, cars mumble and rock in their places; the voices of the people picking through his belongings fade, their bones move, talk to each other. A wave ripples through the street, sets up a beat, long and low, a thrum that brings murmurs out of the curbs, leathery voices from sewer grates, keening calls from the streetlights that bend down and sway over cackling debris. And now the houses move and speak, the panels of the sidewalk stomp and clatter, and it all spreads outward, washing over the city until everything is alive in a deafening dissonance, a throng of rising cries that make Wendell reel, until Masoud grabs his arm and tells him come on, come on. They move through this chaos together, and they are gone by the time the Inspectors arrive, scratching their heads while the last fires in Wendell's apartment wither out.

CHAPTER 3

In Which We Go Underground

 A Body

Though it had been in the water for days, it was found not three hours ago, shuffling in the tides of the East River before wrapping itself in the struts of a pier near the Financial District, where commuters sweating stains in their sharp suits pointed at it and called each other on their cell phones. It will make the paper tomorrow because of this. The brokers and bankers are unused to bodies in the water, it is unprofessional. The reporter for the *Post* who investigates the story will have a private laugh over this, for he grew up in the bowed apartments and bleached warehouses near the stink of the Gowanus Canal, a body of water so polluted that when the city installed a propeller at the bottom to push the muck into the East River; the blades churned for three days and broke, and they're still down there, thirty years later. Back when he was naïve, the reporter and his friends walked along the canal to set parts of it on fire, for the flames from that place were strange, pink and deep blue, and they saw bodies in the water all the time. Mob hits, gang victims. Vendettas, suicides, accidents, in varied stages of decay and dismemberment, ballooning, malformed, nibbled by chemicals and whatever unearthly creature could survive there. In his naïveté, the reporter believed that by becoming a reporter, he could bring these nameless deaths to light; newspapers would be aghast to discover how much it happened. He knows now that newspapers are interested only in death on valuable real estate, but he keeps records himself through police monitors and his own investigations. He goes under the bridges, along the canals, in the alleys behind buildings, into Dumpsters, to add entries to his book, *Death in the Five Boroughs*.

"Why did I pick a husband with such a morbid habit?" his wife asks.

"It's not morbid," he insists. "It's dignified. They deserve it, don't they? To outlive themselves? Henry Briller died when he choked on a pretzel in Riverside Park. Siobhan Mackenzie died of the rabies she contracted from a squirrel. Theresa Hale just stopped breathing on the M5 as it passed 132nd Street. They deserve to be written down, don't they? And all those other people who show up at the city morgue without names or relations. They should be recorded somehow, shouldn't they? To be found later?"

Spaceman Blues

But the reporter has never found a body like this. Its plaid shirt sliced off it, it lies bulbous and huge in the pathologist's lab. The pathologist has one knee on the table, hands inside the mass, peering at it through thick lenses and murmuring to herself. Inspectors Salmon and Trout stand behind her, Salmon playing with his upper lip, Trout eating sour cream-and-onion potato chips from a noisy bag. He peeks at the notes the pathologist has written on the examination form, flecked with fluids, but the characters are illegible to him.

The pathologist pulls out her hands, snaps the liquid off her fingertips. "Well, gentlemen," she says, "I've got bad news: I've never examined a body as inconclusive as this one is."

"Is there a chance that it's Manuel?"

"Inspector, I can't even tell what gender it is. Really. Genitalia, secondary sex characteristics, internal organs, bone structure, all completely ambiguous. We can do a karyotype, but that'll take some time. The decomposition doesn't help much, of course, but I've examined cadavers far more decomposed than this and have been able to sex them right away. But that's just the beginning. If you look here . . . In an every-day corpse like yours or mine, the liver occupies most of this area here. It's a large organ, much larger than people give it credit for. But what do you see here, gentlemen?"

Salmon isn't looking. Trout leans over the table, licking his fingers. "I don't know. . . ."

"There's no reason you should. Now let me tell you something exciting. I'm not sure what it is either. Now of course your first guess is intestine, and why not? This substance dribbling out of it certainly looks and smells like half-digested food, maybe cornmeal or some kind of porridge. But that's just a casual guess. It would be irresponsible of me to identify it as such in a report—please be careful with the potato chips, you're really not even supposed to be in here. Anyway, part of the reason, as I said before, could be because of the obvious state of decay. But another part of me—the unscientific part that should have been a B-movie director—thinks this isn't a person. Maybe a pig, or a young cow. Though I would have been able to sex those. Maybe it's one of those crazy animals they're starting to breed upstate, a llama or some kind of boar. Though if this thing is an animal, it's hard to explain why it's wearing a shirt. A plaid shirt."

"How long has it been dead?" Salmon asks.

"A few days. Though given that I can't find anything in the abdomen, maybe more. A lot more."

"Do you know how it died?"

"Actually . . . this may surprise you, but yes. You see here on the neck . . . this meat loaf–like area is where the head should be, but you can tell without my help that it looks like it's been burned off. Not even a few days in the river could hide this."

Trout is finishing his chips. "How intense was the heat?"

"Very intense. Like an explosion. Incineration."

Trout smiles. "Perhaps it is as I suspected." He turns to Salmon. "This is about a great thing moving below us, now and again showing us a flip of fin, a side of scales. This is a larger story. It is a story written across the face of our city, a story about sparks, a story about fires."

"No," Salmon says, "This is a story about three people, two missing, one dead. So far, there is nothing else."

"The explosions were real."

"The explosions don't matter. The people do."

"Humanist."

"Reptile."

"Gentlemen, gentlemen, lower your voices, remember you're not supposed to be here?"

"Of course you're right, Doctor . . ."

"Indira Gore."

"Dr. G—"

"—Yes, that's right, please don't bother with jokes or surprise. It could be worse. I know a Dr. Slaughter who's a surgeon. Now if you have no more questions?"

They exchange cards, handshakes. Gore's hand is humid and powdered from the glove, and later, Trout finds himself moving his fingers over his palm, bringing his hand up to his face. The tart smell of latex comes first, then passes; then there is a faint floral air, carrying lilies, sweet and full.

"You liked her," Salmon says.

"She is clever and bears her unfortunate moniker with grace."

". . ."

"Be quiet."

The bulletin board behind Salmon's desk is a quarter full now. Pictures of Manuel, pictures of Wendell. A note tacked in the corner, *Masoud Azzi?*, because he didn't answer his phone when they called. Testimony of something flying. Photographs of blasted ruins, the bones of furniture, black floors, boiled ceilings, walls splayed with ash. Salmon returns again and again to these pictures, looking for traces of people in their tattered shapes. He read too much about Hiroshima and Nagasaki at an impressionable age, knows how a blast drives dust into concrete, clothing patterns into the skin below, the shadow of a man into the wall behind him. You can see in his posture if he had enough time to run. Oh, he believes forensics when they say there's no way that Manuel or Wendell were in their apartments when the bombs went off. We would have found a body, they say, some of a body, anyway. But he imagines that one night he'll be fog-eyed, staring at those pictures, and the fluorescent bulbs will flicker to reveal the outlines of men, throwing their hands over their faces or lunging for the door, the pristine shape of a coffee cup that never made it to the floor. All etched in plaster by flame.

"The man is alive," Trout keeps saying. Yes, yes, alive and part of something large and important. But maybe Salmon doesn't want that. Maybe he wants it simpler: three men died in fires and were mourned by their friends and family. He thinks of Lucy Rutman. You think too much, he tells Trout, then winces, waiting for Trout's inevitable reply: maybe you're not thinking enough.

 Y'all Ready for This?

Wendell and Masoud are clinging to the top of a garbage truck, and it is aloft, tilting in the air, tracing a tail of dirt and debris. The Marsupials are in the cab, fighting. Mammoth George on the passenger side holds Slinky's head out the window, while

Asshole and Kenny Jim wrestle for control of the steering wheel. Even from the top of the truck, through the wind and howls, Wendell can hear Sly and the Family Stone thumping from the speakers, and as the truck noses down into the river, he has time to think.

It has been forty-two hours since his apartment exploded; there was a stop of twenty-seven minutes for Masoud to gather a flashlight, two batteries, a first aid kit, a picture of his family, and a pack of Lucky Strikes. He hauled two crates into the basement, propped the window open. Then it was off to the old World's Fair grounds, where Masoud said a contact lived. They waited until four in the morning under the flying saucers; planes screamed overhead and floated into LaGuardia while teenagers smoked pot and fornicated on the wet lawns and a walleyed security guard patrolled the grounds, took bribes. At last the contact arrived through a manhole she lifted with a pneumatic jack. No, she didn't know where Manuel was, though she'd heard he was leaving.

"Do you know a place," Wendell said, "called . . . the city of the dark? La . . . crap, *la ciudad de . . .*"

"You mean Darktown?" she said.

"Yes, yes, Darktown. Darktown. Where lost things are found."

"Never heard of it," she said. "You should find the Marsupials? An Australian pop band from the eighties, had a hit in China with 'Don't Try to Box (A Kangaroo)?' They don't do music anymore. They play the currency market and smuggle computer components from India to the United States, sell them at staggering markups. They'll take you there. They'll take you anywhere."

The Marsupials met Manuel three years ago in a bar under a wharf in Carpinteria, after they'd just arrived, bruisers from Oz with too much money on their hands. When they bought the fourth round of drinks, the men with mustaches, stilettos, and forty-fives suspected their wealth, got ideas. This was just what the Marsupials wanted: as soon as the blades came out, the band was breaking glasses, swinging chairs. The bartender saw this, wiped his hands on a towel, and walked out just as Slinky and Mammoth George were thrown laughing through the window. They were having a blast. They did not realize the mustaches were serious until Kenny Jim and Asshole were stabbed in the gut and slumped against the wall, surprised and leaking blood and bile. It would have killed them if not for Manuel, who emerged from the bathroom and stood on the bar, told everyone to calm down or else; then he stabilized Asshole and Kenny Jim with tequila and the bartender's towel until the paramedics arrived. After that, the Marsupials thought they owed Manuel. It did not occur to them that he had reasons for doing what he did: it was a show of power, the ability to control a room, and outside the place, the men in silk and linen suits looked at each other and nodded. He was gone before the Marsupials could thank him; but they saw him again a year and a half later, stepping off a freight train in New Jersey. His hair was shorter, he'd grown a little beard, but Asshole and Kenny Jim recognized the eyes, the hands that had saved them.

"Thank you," they said.

"No offense," Manuel said, "but please don't act like you know who I am." They would never see him again.

Wendell and Masoud looked for them in the onion dome of St. Nicholas on 97th Street, where it was said they'd lived; they looked in the ornate ironworked fire escapes on the buildings along Bayard. They found them, at last, on the High Line, the grassy spine of overgrown tracks shooting through Hell's Kitchen. The Marsupials were walking four abreast and harmonizing the ballad from what had always been their favorite cut from their album, despite its disastrous showing in the charts. Who's Manuel? Kenny Jim said. Stupid git, said Slinky, he's the geezer who—right, right. No, they hadn't seen him, but they knew who might have.

"In Darktown?" Wendell said.

The four of them exchanged uncomfortable looks.

"Are you sure you want to go there?" Slinky said. "Been there before?"

"No. But I saw it, through a hole in the floor in Washington Heights."

"Going down there doesn't narrow it down, see, if you're looking for someone."

"It's a big place," Mammoth George said.

"Very big," Slinky said.

"Perhaps worse," Asshole said, "the news that you're there, looking for your man, might attract some . . . unsavory characters to the vicinity of your person."

"Kind of man he was," Kenny Jim said.

"What do you mean?"

"How do we mean, you say?" Slinky said. "Well, you knew

him, the kind of trouble he got himself into. Helped us more than a few times, of course, he could get a herd of elephants into this country and back out again and nobody who didn't need to know would be any the wiser. Still. Dangerous fellow. Willing to deal with people that we, well—"

"—That we would not want to deal with in a business sort of way," Mammoth George said.

"War criminals, say," Asshole said. "Out of Central America, Central Africa. Yugoslavia or what's left of it. People whose childhood memories consist of pouring gasoline to help burn villages down."

"Like El Flaco . . ."

"El Flaco?" Slinky said, flattening the *a* and rounding the *o*. "El Flaco's a fucking country gentleman compared to those people. He wouldn't touch them, wouldn't deal with them."

"Manuel's working with them was all on the side," Kenny Jim said. "Things El Flaco didn't know about, see. He did a lot of things El Flaco didn't know about."

Asshole snickers.

"Begging your pardon, of course," Kenny Jim said.

"What kinds of things was he smuggling—"

"—Oh, now there's a dirty word, smuggling. We're distributors in the informal economy." Slinky said. "But Manuel, Christ, Manuel moved whatever he could. Drugs, of course—who doesn't move drugs—but he went across the world and back again for that. People, of course, that's El Flaco's racket. But then other things too. Arms. Missiles. Nuclear weapons sometimes, now there's a brisk trade. He'd move anything, that was his reputation at least, it was why people came to him, and he never let them down, well, as far as I know he never did. *El coyote mejor,* El Flaco used to say. He was so proud of Manuel, used to brag about him."

"Before all that nonsense with Lavinia," Mammoth George said. "Now he wants to kill him."

"Look, see here," Slinky said. "We're just small-timers in this world. We do illegal, but not dangerous. We like a good fight from time to time, when we get to lose a tooth or two—*shhhhh!*" At the mention of fights, Asshole and Mammoth George had started elbowing each other in the ribs and giggling; they shut up.

"But Manuel," Slinky said. "He was into things. Things I could not even guess at. The news he's disappeared's gone three times round the globe and back by now. If you want to find him, you'd better do it fast, because you won't be the only one looking. And some of those other people will not be friendly."

"Not that we couldn't take them in a friendly tussle—," Asshole said.

"—Shut *up,*" Kenny Jim said.

"Who knows?" Slinky said. "Maybe if you make enough of a nuisance of yourself, they'll come looking for you too?"

Of course the Mafia helicopter had to come then. It had been tracking the Marsupials since they forgot to cover the evidence of their last major sale. Mobsters following their trail realized who they were dealing with, tax evasion, fraud, libel, coercion, butting in on their turf, nothing intimidation or death couldn't fix. They brought in the knuckle breakers from Long Island and Jersey, set up offices in abandoned warehouses in the Meatpacking District, and waited until this moment, this very moment, to strike, battering in from overhead, stop right where you are, buddy. The Marsupials grabbed Wendell and Masoud and fled off the tracks and behind angled apartment buildings on 39th Street, hijacked a garbage truck in which they careened down the West Side Highway, crashed through a cyclone fence, barreled off a pier and into the air. That's where Wendell is now, thinking of all this as the water tilts toward him, then smacks him in the face and parts with a roar.

The garbage truck descends through the water, the strains of Sly still warbling from the cab, the image of the helicopter warping in the waves above. Soon all sound falls away, and they are moving where it is dark and cool. Asshole and Kenny Jim are thinking about their vision quest in the outback after the money started coming in, just them and an army-rejected desert vehicle and two suitcases full of peyote they'd imported from Arizona. Slinky is thinking about the dreams he used to have of outer space, the ache he used to feel at not having been born three thousand years later on a planet where the Orion Nebula explodes the night sky in monstrous swaths of blue and purple and orange, oh, the things their descendants would see. Mammoth George is soaking in the moment, he realizes that he will remember this, the feel of the plastic seats on his fat back and the Hudson all around him; when he is eighty-seven years old, phlegmatic and rheumatoid, he will remember. Masoud is back in Beirut, and Wendell for some reason thinks of the day when his father stopped following him, a summer day hiking along a lost stretch of the New River with a preacher who told him surely this was God's country, and maybe it was, for he felt his father go from him, down into the rocks along the shore, into the water, the soil at his feet. It wasn't good-bye; it was a truce, a promise that the peace would come later. But it has not.

The helicopter is gone by the time they surface, it didn't have clearance to be in city airspace and saw the police choppers coming. The squad cars haven't arrived yet; they're still snaking through side streets, trying to get around moving trucks, buses, delivery vans, they won't get here for eleven minutes. So the six of them wring the water from their clothes as best they can, pour the sludge from their shoes, and start walking.

"So you'll take us there," Wendell says.

"To Darktown?" Kenny Jim says. "Of course. We live there."

". . . can't believe they just found us like that," Asshole says. "We'll be able to start something big now . . ."

". . . *shhhhh* . . .," says Mammoth George, and puts a wide finger to his lips.

A century ago, the shores of Manhattan thronged with ships, the piers bloated with sailors and wares and the dreams of women and dead boys, and the freight rails ran in droves down the west side of the island, bringing in goods, taking out goods; the tracks were lines of food and wealth that, during the Depression, grew thick with shantytowns and roving workers dying to grab a piece. Soon the air reeked of feces and desire, hunger strong enough to break horses. The landed complained; the authorities tried spreading dissent in the camps, they tried to bust the squatters out of there, but they would not go. At last, the government built stone shells around the tracks and buried the shantytown in piles of earth, rock outcroppings, planted it over with grass and trees, lined it with walkways and stone balconies, and called it Riverside Park. But the trains still ran, the food and wealth was still there, so people still went to live in that dark shelter under the gardens, cobblestones, and dog runs, they lined the sides of the tunnels with houses first of cardboard and pressed Styrofoam, then bricks and plaster. They began to burrow deeper. They dug into the soil that had displaced their grandfathers, they broke boulders, they drilled into bedrock. At night they dynamited, hollowed out great spaces, and began to move in there, by the hundreds, by the thousands. The trains stopped, the entrance was boarded up, but by then there were hundreds of other entrances; the people had already torched holes out of the ceilings of drainage pipes, smashed them out of the basements of buildings and the back ends of alleys, installed hatches under the benches in the parks, put hinges on manholes. There were hundreds of ways down in the walls of subway tunnels, and the people kept coming. They stole construction equipment and jackhammered deeper, they kept going until they hit the water table and the floor flooded; then they brought in boats, rafts, anything that would float, hung their dwellings from the ceiling by steel cables, connected it all with ladders and chains. They built a civilization down there and they called it Darktown.

"Welcome under," Slinky says.

They enter from under a false Dumpster, inch down a tunnel that begins as a crawlspace but widens and widens, gathering light and sound until it ends at a metal platform Wendell recognizes as a stolen fire escape, mounted halfway up the wall of a vast cavern suffused with an ochre glow that lets him see. Darktown is gigantic. He had no idea it could be so big, that there could be so much space here, so many *people*. Catwalks and narrow metal stairs sway and tangle, metal shacks and globular houses hang suspended in the air, floating bars and restaurants throw out heat and steam, thousands of people climb with bundles on their backs and lights lashed to their heads, shouts and whistles fly across the space, animals scramble amok, babies scream, a riot of music threatens to resolve into a deep, smoky rhythm that shudders and moans. High above, the exposed pipes of the city heating system lance along the cavern ceiling, spouting steam. The belly of a subway tunnel shifts as a train rattles by, looses a film of dust that falls through all this, settling on the heads of the multitude, sprinkling through the latticework to rest, at last, on the water below that teems with boats, people rowing, trundling along with grunting engines. They're selling things from Bangladesh and Brazil, they have the teeth of a hundred beasts not yet named, they have rice cookers and machine guns, blowtorches and flares. It smells of fish, oil, and burnt electrical wire, a scent that trails through the people and light and sounds, to the arms of the city that they can see only as a group of yellow lights, like the shine of dull suns in constellation, dim but carrying for miles.

"It stretches under all of Manhattan," Mammoth George says, "down to the thirties. Then, again, under Brooklyn and Queens, into the Bronx. A little up into Westchester and on into Nassau County. They tried to build it under the Financial District, but the buildings were too tall, too heavy. Dangerous."

"How many people . . . ," Masoud says.

"Don't know. Five millions? Seven . . ."

"It's the city all over again," Asshole says. "The city inside-out . . ."

"There's this feeling I used to get," Kenny Jim says, waxing oracular, "when I lived on the surface, some nights, when the boys ran mad, crashing into each other, making mischief in all-night delis, and the couples kissed up against the dark storefronts, and the cops were sleeping on the beat, and inside the clubs and bars you could hear the music, just throbbing, until the doors opened and the people flew out of there like they'd been under pressure, laughing and screaming, the sound got loud enough to kill you, and the wind came whipping down the street like a pack of wild ponies, threw trash and papers spiraling into the sky . . . those nights when things were feral again, crackling and lethal and howling, those nights I could feel the planet moving under my feet, groaning on its axis, moving through its orbit, and I felt a part of it, all of it, like I was dissolving into that gorgeous chaos . . . well, that's this place, mate. Twenty-four hours down here and you almost never want to go back up."

They climb down to a pier of splintered railroad ties reinforced by I-beams. Two boats are tied to it. One appears to be mounded high with cocaine and is surrounded by armed guards in Bolivian combat gear with greasy Uzis. The other has been welded together from chopped-up pieces of other boats; it is rusty and empty save for its captain, who lounges outside the cabin, legs propped against the rail, smoking a long clove cigarette.

"Captain McHeath," Asshole calls.

"Fuck off," she says.

Asshole digs into his pants and produces a plastic bag ballooning with hashish. It lands with a sodden plop near her head.

"What do you want?"

"These fine people are looking for someone," Asshole says. "Need information, chop-chop."

"We need to go to Under Hell Gate," Mammoth George says.

"Let me guess," she says. "To Hyrvygeena."

They nod.

Without getting up, she lifts the bag in her hand, tosses it, catches it.

"This is more than fair price for that. And I don't have any change." A languid hand passes over the empty boat.

"Let's just consider you owe us something," Asshole says.

"I don't owe you anything."

She starts the outboard and the boat growls awake, leaks oil into the water, and soon they are trundling under the web of houses. It is a swamp of metal. Ladders dangle into the water, the bottom rungs are covered with fungus. Above, a party starts on a rickety platform, a dozen people and a rusty keg with a radio duct-taped to the side, hip-hop stepping out of it, voices that sing *my people, my people.* . . . In the boat, the Marsupials are holding Asshole by his legs, they're dipping him into the water up to his waist. He comes up with key rings in his mouth, an old shirt, a creature with nine legs that bites him on the inside of the cheek and raises a large red welt. He spits it into the boat; there is a commotion of shouting and stomping until Mammoth George fixes the thing under his boot and crushes it, hard shell and all. They then debate whether to eat it.

The boats ahead clot around a smear of light and sound, and Captain McHeath slows the engine. "Darktown Market . . . ," she says.

The greasy glow and clamoring voices burst into a flotilla of rafts and punts with small huts built on them, cauldrons and kettles, counters and stools made from oil drums, frying pans fashioned from galvanized sheet metal and engine parts glinting under kerosene. Long calls from cooks, the constant clatter of cutlery, frantic atonal runs from a piercing, nasal reed instrument somewhere, the cries of animals being slaughtered, and now the air is thick with smoke and steam, the smells of seventy-two spices, vegetables, offal, blood. The boat pulls up alongside a pier of pallets nailed together and buoyed by Styrofoam; they are mobbed by ragged people with lanterns on posts attached to their heads, jostling among vendors shouting the names of their wares, batteries, bullets, lighters, electric toys, cyanide. . . . Under the shadow of a gigantic concrete strut ribbed with rebar, Darktown Market is a sprawling, rickety lattice of I-beams and chains, the welded sides of railroad cars, cinder blocks, and stretched canvas that metastasizes up from the water to the ceiling above. The water is thronging with boats—junks, skiffs, rafts of corrugated metal and scrap wood tied together with twine—and their pilots are calling in aggressive melody, rifle rifle rifle, used car parts, get your puppies here, computahs, computahs, day labor day labor day labor. A swarm of words in a hundred other languages. Letters blare in neon and half-burnt lightbulbs: *Beer, Radios Sold and Repaired; Documents Forged and Sold; Dr. Ease's Drug Emporium, Pharmaceuticals of All Varieties,* jammed amid Spanish signs, Chinese and Korean characters, the shapes of the Cyrillic alphabet, other symbols Wendell cannot identify. Mountains of clothes and shoes, people waist-deep in them. A woman with a tall black boot in one hand, looking for its mate. Mounds of vegetables, crates of sweet, acrid fruit; butchered animals hanging on nails from their legs, skinned and draining and swarmed with flies, the butchers hack off cuts with machetes and wrap the meat in five-year-old newspapers. Brown tubes of fluorescent lights, blinking and buzzing; lanterns swing on long ropes when the structure shakes, candles tip over and start small fires that are then put out with old pighair rugs. Virile dogs and children bite and tumble, boys jostle with carts and wheelbarrows, and the space swells with the chatter of haggling, the bark of a thousand vendors, the rushing and collapsing of jangling music that resolves into a pulse, a groove, a thumping motion. A heart.

They arrive at a platform floating on stained oil drums. A chain ladder ascends to a graffiti-smothered subway car hanging from bridge cables, a painted sign on the bottom illuminated by a border of yellow lightbulbs: *Hyrvygeena*. The Marsupials leap to the ladder before the boat has docked and clamber up giggling like kindergartners. Asshole whispers fight fight fight, is hit again by Mammoth George. McHeath ties up, resumes her position, feet up, arms folded behind her head. She lets the Marsupials get a lead, then stops Wendell and Masoud with a snap of her fingers.

"Hey. It's all big fun to them, you know, just a huge playground," she says. "When you find out what you want to know, get out. As fast as you can. Those people you're with? Forget them. You deserve to die in a better place than this."

The first time she met Manuel, he bent his head and leaned into her ear, said something dirty in Spanish that angered her and made her swoon. They were in a green metal trailer fixed to the belly of a coughing boiler in Under Midtown, and the party had decayed into duels with power tools and yelling about women. No one noticed when she brought her lips to his neck, or when they opened the window and slipped out, slid down ladders through the oily air to her boat; she untied it and they let it float. She knew about his other lovers, did not mind. He bounced among them, an iron spark on a cement floor, but she was the magnet, she thought, cooling him down, pulling him in. She played a game in which she told no one where she was going, took her boat into the caves at the end of Darktown where the water came from and the light stopped, to the coves under the George Washington Bridge. She left it tied to the piers in the market, climbed among the houses until she was lost and went to sleep on a metal platform in an unmarked place. He always found her, called her name in the dark, woke her with his hands. She began to think she'd have him for decades, considered children, until one night three men dragged him from the hold of her boat and broke four of his ribs with a crowbar.

"Who were they?" she said.

Manuel tried to laugh, but his ribs hurt too much. "Two cousins and an uncle."

"Who were they?" she said.

Then Manuel spoke in a voice laden with lizard menace, a voice that frightened her.

"Stay away from it," he said. "It is not for you."

"Are you threatening me?" she said.

"Stay away," he said. "I will not ask again."

She made him go the next day, sank the clothes he left behind in the water. She heard that he was spending more time above, that he found someone else, a man, a man who didn't even know they were down here. And now here he is, his face wrinkled with quiet terror, enslaved by a thing she recognizes. I know what is in you, she wants to say. You don't have to go so far. But she understands it is useless to speak. She turns the bag of hashish in her hands and makes no move to smoke it.

 Good at Dodgeball

For the last three months, Lucas has had intense flashbacks to his cultish childhood. Small things trigger them: the smell of a brand of soap takes him back to the communal showers, where he lost his virginity to a forty-year-old woman whose husband had died two weeks before. It was an act of grief for her, an act of forgetting, while he scrambled to master the mechanics of his hips. A mailman on a sitcom pulls him into the days when a reporter from a regional newspaper broke into the compound and shot six rolls of film before he was caught and drugged, his film shredded. Even at that age, Lucas thought of the constitutional rights he'd been taught by the Founder's second daughter. Freedom of speech? Freedom of the press? The Founder laughed. These are the laws of man, he said. They have no place in the Temple's work. Ma Xiao Ling blames the FBI's deprogramming regime for Lucas's triggered memories. If they'd left you alone, she says, you probably would not be so maladjusted. She's been studying the dictionary, is more comfortable with long words than most native speakers are. Robert Lord Townsend slaps him on the back, says he's a regular Proust, and Lucas resents the allusion, stifles the urge to beat him senseless. That's just a book, he says. This is my life.

There was a time after the deprogramming sessions when he felt like he was made of leaves. The wind blew pieces of him away, they drifted to North Dakota, to the dried-up beds of dead rivers. One flame and he would burn. All around him appeared chaotic, ready to explode; any minute now, he thought, the trees will fly apart in a swarm of splinters, the bricks will jump from their mortar, the sea will rise and take us all. Over time, order was restored, he saw patterns in the splay of flower petals and the flow of traffic. But his faith did not return. He hated the Founder for the lies he had told, but he missed that feeling, the sense that the world was holy, that there was a plan.

Despite his faithlessness, though, he exudes the aura of one who has seen. Fundamentalist Christians and Jews for Jesus do not single him out on the subway as a man in need of saving. They sit across from him, throw him knowing smiles, talk to him as to their own. He can speak the language, he calls them all his brothers and sisters, he remembers all the epithets his parents taught him. Go in peace, he says, and does not think of them again.

While waiting for the bus on Van Brunt, he is accosted by three members of the Church of Panic, floating down the sidewalk in flowing robes of black and white. Lucas knows them, knows in fact their High Epopt, a childhood friend who fled the Lunar Temple with his family at the age of eight, eating his own snot. Good at dodgeball, smart, though he had trouble remembering longer prayers. The trio slides by him, chanting, then stops, wheels around, and approaches.

"We know you," they say in unison.

Lucas nods his head in a brotherly way.

"Do you know when they are coming?"

"I do not, brothers, but I await the day." It is so natural to him.

"The Day is almost here."

"Praise be."

"No, no, you do not comprehend. The Day is almost here. Next month, three weeks from now."

"I have seen the signs in the sky, brother."

"Then you have seen almost nothing of what is coming. Look." From his robes, the leader produces a long silver scroll. Lowering himself to the ground, he gets down on his hands and knees and unrolls it on the sidewalk. It is a long column of numbers. The man points to a set that seems anomalous, is much higher than the ones around it.

"Here. Here. Do you understand?"

"No . . . what is this I'm looking at?"

"Data from the National Aeronautics and Space Administration's routine monitoring of the near solar system."

"I beg your pardon?"

"You . . . you do not understand? Even now?"

"No . . . understand what, no . . ."

The leader grows angry, turns to his followers. "This man is a pretender. He knows nothing. Disengage your believing tone, my friend, and begin stocking food. The Day is at hand."

Lucas thinks of how many times he heard that as a child. Those words slapped him from sleep, piercing through the loudspeaker at the center of the compound, the Founder's voice edged with razors. The Day is at hand; his legs would not work, his parents had to take him by both arms and drag him outside where the families had already gathered, already they were up on tiptoes, lips puckered. It was the strongest memory his childhood gave him, standing like that for hours in the dark while the Right Hands of the Founder circled the group with billy clubs. Discipline, they said in even voices, for the Day is at hand. He must have heard it hundreds of times, but it was never accompanied by data from NASA. He tilts his head to the glaring sky. It is blank and cloudless, a flat, burning blue that offers no pattern, gives no sign of the things to come.

Green Flame

The subway car that houses Hyrvygeena was in service for twenty years, running the 2 line from 241st Street in the Bronx to Flatbush Avenue in Brooklyn, in the days when the rich believed the subways were death traps for their kind. Do not go on them after dark, they said, they are filled with weapons, they are vectors for disease. In 1979, there was an accidental death on it: a man doing pull-ups on the straphangers' bar fell when the train jostled, landed on his head and provoked an aneurysm that had been building in his skull, undetected, for years. In 1981, the car received a graffito that stretched from end to end, depicting a view of Manhattan as seen from a quarter mile up, fisheyed so that the streets bulged away, buildings curled, splayed open, the skyscrapers in the distance lanced up at vertiginous angles. The yawning perspective induced nausea in some, but the graffiti artists shook their spray cans and said it was a masterpiece. Hackerin' Pete agreed: he stole the car off the tracks a year later, varnished it to preserve the paint, and strung it from the cavern's ceiling in Under Hell Gate, at the time just mushroom farms. He bolted the light sockets to the bottom, hung the ladder down to the water as the city crawled around him and the air grew dense with floating houses. In 1986, tremors that nobody on the surface felt almost destroyed all of Darktown; two of the cables supporting Hyrvygeena snapped, screamed as they whipped back. The car groaned and yawed, twenty-two people fell out of the doors and spun down through space, broke their heads open on jutting metal, plunged into the water and were dragged to the bottom by falling debris. Hackerin' Pete never managed to hang Hyrvygeena straight after that, and now it's at an angle; spilled glasses roll down the floor, and at the end of the night the low side of the place is a trough of beer and sticky wine glazed with whiskey and peppered with cigarette ash, all draining out of holes Hackerin' Pete drilled in the floor. He has photographs of the earthquake damage, shots of wrenched beams and people weeping, he has portraits of the twenty-two when they were still alive, smiling, drinking, hands wrapped around their mouths and calling out. The pictures are on the wall of the car, next to the scratched and broken windows and the ads for *Torn Earlobe?* and Dr. Zizmor behind the bar. To the twenty-two, Hackerin' Pete says, and opens twenty-two bottles of whiskey; you only get to drink if you know what he's talking about.

Hyrvygeena is always packed: without the sun, the boys never know when to go home. The Marsupials thread through fast. Within a minute, Masoud has some African beer in his hand and Wendell has a green cocktail in which the bubbles somehow move downward.

"I do not recommend drinking that," Masoud says. In the corner, two men start shouting at each other; one breaks the leg off a chair and starts beating the other with it, while a third man explains that they're old friends, they do this all the time. Over the din, Wendell can hear the voices of the Marsupials cutting through, bloke over there, yeah. Yeah. Looking for Manuel. Right over there, with the bubbly drink. He looks at Masoud, whose eyes pass over this crowd, there's a tension in the pilot's arms that suggests a punch a blink away from realization. Don't fuck with us, it says. But heads are turning toward them all the same, appraising them. They've got their calipers on him and have figured him out fast: newcomer, whitebread, what did Manuel see in him . . .

"You should shut them boys up," an old man says behind him. "It's not good that they should say so much so fast. . . . Oh, no need to introduce yourself, half the bar knows who you are. You not sure you ain't fucking with us when you say you don't know where he is?"

Wendell is still working through the triple negative. ". . . Y—no . . ."

"Well, hell. Another theory shot to shit. See, I thought for sure he'd gone upstairs for good and that's why nobody knew where he was. It's like I told my girl, I said, Abigail, I said, he's topside in the sun now and you won't never see him. I fancied him in a condo in the sky, out on the balcony, looking down over that river, all across Brooklyn and Queens, and in your arms. That's what I fancied. . . ."

His drone is lost in the squeal of a mike, the pop of guitars being plugged in. The crowd throws out shouts, whoops, a voice yells *fucking play already* . . .

"—Thanks, people, thanks. You know how much we like playing here." The bass thumps: it's the Pan-Galactic Groove

Squad assembling on the stage, the percussionists are testing their congas, bringing their palms down on djembes, they're ready to go.

"...know you really should get those Marsupials to shut their traps," the old man says, "because them boys in raincoats been coming by—"

"—Raincoats?"

"Oh yes. Looking for you, looking for...well, seems they've got a long list of people, anyone who they think was close to your boyfriend. They ask about you all the time. Heh. Course nobody in the place even knew what you looked like, never seen you before in their lives, well not before tonight. Not that it would've made a difference. Folks in here, they wouldn't turn you over, hell, half the people in here hiding from something or another. Some of them are hiding from each other, come in here different nights saying don't tell them you saw me here. But them boys in the raincoats is different. They ain't giving up...now come in close and let me tell you why I'm talking to you."

The guitar peels out a riff and the horns jump on it, the drums leap into the pocket, and the Groove Squad is off. The old man coughs and puts his mouth to Wendell's ear.

"I don't know who put you on the Marsupials, but you get off them quick, you hear me? All this talking they doing, it's putting the word out you're here, it's going to bring the boys in raincoats screaming in here from God knows where they're from. See, the Marsupials, they do shit just to piss people off, just to start fights with them. But those raincoat boys. Son. The Marsupials don't know what kind of fire they playing with."

Somebody's tapping on Wendell's shoulder; it's Masoud and he points to the band, who are playing the happiest music he's ever heard them play but they're all looking at him with terrified faces. Two of the percussionists are moving their mouths in unison, they're trying to say something that Wendell understands without hearing, get out, get out . . .

"Run, boy," the old man says. "Run until your feet bleed."

Too late: there is a sound from outside like jet engines; then four hulking shapes squeeze through the door, fan out at the entrance to block escape. The band crashes to a stop, but they're good enough to make it artful, the horns blare a final chord over a drumroll, and there is silence in the place, but for the sloshing of the trough and some loud fucker who still hasn't gotten with the program.

". . . And the octopus says, *play* it?" he yells. "As soon as I—" and then he's quiet, shushed by his neighbors.

The raincoated heads regard the crowd.

"Where is Apogee?" the first one says, in a hoarse voice laced with a high-pitched, amorphous squeal like feedback. "We have heard the man is here."

Nobody moves. Nobody looks at Wendell. The whole room is covering for him.

"Which of you is Apogee?" the giant says.

"Here he is," says Asshole, standing up and pointing at himself.

"And here," Mammoth George rises to his stout legs.

"And me too, you fucking wanker," Slinky says. It's their Spartacus moment.

The giants start reaching into their raincoats for something, but before they can finish, the Marsupials are on them, pummeling and kicking. The giants let out a collective shriek that rattles glass; Slinky is thrown through the air and crashes into the back wall, twitches on the ground once, and is on his feet and attacking again, leaving teeth on the floor. People are diving under tables, they wrestle through the fray, trying to reach the doors, which for some reason have chosen to reactivate and are chiming and closing, opening, chiming and closing, opening. Mammoth George holds his ground: feet fixed, he lays about him with a wooden chair, knocking his enemies to the floor, catching them on the head to make them spin once and collapse.

Hackerin' Pete pulls a shotgun from behind the bar, he's about to tell everyone to calm the fuck down, but he's not ready for what's coming: with a metallic cry, the first giant produces a device that takes two seconds to warm up and then throws a crackling jet of green flame across the room. Everyone hits the floor, the people under the table huddle closer, cover their heads. They only hear the weapon discharge again, then yelps and crashes, sounds of panting, of breaking wood.

Masoud is dragging Wendell toward the door. Wendell protests, I can do it myself, but then sees it's no use, the former soldier in Masoud has taken over, it's in the stretch of sinew, the turn of his head. Mammoth George is bludgeoning one of the giants with a table; it takes aim, misses, and torches a long gash in the roof that sets the suspension cables to singing. For a second, the whole car creaks and lurches, and then the cable snaps, the car angles down, and Wendell and Masoud slide out the door in a tumble of customers and demolished furniture. Wendell spins three times before he hits the water; he sees Hyrvygeena cockeyed and shuddering, shooting green flame, the Marsupials still wrestling inside. Around him, men and women falling. Below, Captain McHeath's boat, engine roaring, she was ready to go all along, and then the black water. He has enough time to think, *Christ, twice in one day,* before a beer mug hits him, his head swells, and he's gone.

 ## Wendell's Dream #2

He is in a glass bubble, descending into a purple sea exploding with green fish that swirl around the sphere in a seething fire. The surface is far above, but the light does not diminish; no, all is washed in lavender here, huge crags of coral glisten with crustaceans, lorded over by knobby sharks and vast expanses of open water where humpbacks hover and sing the blues. He passes derelict ships still sailing on submarine currents, older boats, the ribs of triremes, snagged on crops of rock. Golden spider crabs seventeen feet across stilt around a swarm of clicking young, they dine on the carcass of a sperm whale large enough to be a landform, a great hill overgrown with teeming greens. At last, Wendell settles on the ridge of a blinding abyss, where Manuel lives inside the giant mouth of a fossilized squid. Manuel has learned to breathe water, his heart pushes brine through his veins, the movement of the sea along the ocean floor passes through his head. He approaches the bubble, puts his hands upon the surface, presses his forehead against it, writes with a curved finger: I'm sorry. And Wendell puts his lips against the cold curve over Manuel's eyes, moves across his beloved's forehead, his limbs collapse against the glass, just trying to get closer; but it is no use. Above him, the whales are gathering, preparing for migration: they know of a stretch of ocean that is warmer and brighter than this place, where the current teems with sweet krill and there are no hunters in rusting ships trying to kill them. But it is thousands of miles away. It could take years to get there.

|CHAPTER 4|

In Which a Death Is Faked,
and Church Membership Grows

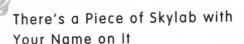 There's a Piece of Skylab with
Your Name on It

The night crew on the runway at JFK is going mad. They drive
off the tarmac at dawn, eyes raving; they draw diagrams on the
skin of their arms, a dense web of lines that nobody can un-
tangle. They wave their hands in strange patterns, speak of the
sky slit open and peeled back, and beyond, all is waves of liquid fire, a planet full of voices rising in unison, the clanging of
a million gongs, while they lie below, mouths open, hacking
out ragged breaths.

The Ecuadorians look at each other and nod. They know

how the madness comes. Behind a plane, the air screams and flies apart, but the air in front is almost silent, the plane's nose slips through it almost without sound, so that an aircraft can approach without you noticing. Over the growl of boats in the bay and the cries of seagulls, you hear the engines like the stirring of trees, it might not even occur to you to turn around, but if you do, you'll see the impossible hulk of the plane descending upon you. It may already be too late then; but if it is not, you're flat out, face down, pissing yourself on the runway while the engines tear the atmosphere to pieces. They are angels of destruction, the night crew says, and the Ecuadorians understand: before they worked there, it was unbelievable that something so big could move with such speed and silence, rushing in behind you while you stood there with a toolbox, oblivious. They say three near misses unhinge you. You start to feel colossi bearing down on you everywhere you go. You maneuver down the street with shopping bags while buildings crash behind you, the street itself falls away, satellites and space stations careen out of near orbit, spiral toward your head.

The Ecuadorians have had two near misses, one with a DC-10, the other with a 737. In both cases, their collectivity saved them. The first one who saw it shouted to the others, and they locked arms as the plane passed over them so that the engines would not eat them. They feel no closer to insanity now, feel no anxiety, no, not after what they passed through to get here. They do not remember leaving Ecuador, the *coyote* who told their parents he could take them to Los Angeles, then stranded them in Guatemala. But they can recall fleeing into the hills with their mothers and sisters while the soliders massacred the men in front of the church, then burned everything, smoothed out the ash, took the village's name off the map. They remember the long march through the jungle, across the border into Mexico, a cousin dying of malaria, writhing and insane, the mother wailing because there was no way to bury her. Work in cornfields. Work in onyx mines, boulders riding their backs. Working their way north from town to town, starving themselves and saving, looking gaunt and criminal when they met Manuel in Baja, the Pacific booming against the rocks below while the police rounded up a gang of amateur smugglers. Sure, I can get you into Los Estados Unidos, Manuel said. Anywhere you want to go. San Diego. San Francisco. There is work in Lincoln, Nebraska, they need hands to build homes. New York.

The four of them looked at each other. "We want to go to New York," they said.

Manuel smiled. "Everyone wants to go to New York," he said.

They spent a week packed into a freight car with eighty other people. Six of them began to believe they were cattle, regurgitated what was in their stomachs, sucked it off their shirts and swallowed it again. Eight others died of heat stroke; their bodies were unloaded in Virginia and slipped into the Chesapeake. When the train spat them out in New Jersey and they walked across the George Washington Bridge into Manhattan, they looked like old men, and Lázaro had suffered kidney damage that would take eight years off his life, though he would never know the difference. Now the criminals on the subway, the threat of traffic accidents, the landing of planes cannot frighten them. Their bodies are callused, muscles taut, even when they sleep. They are heroes on the soccer field. But just yesterday, they were fixing lights along the runway and looked over the expanse of the airfield, a featureless plane blank enough to bring vertigo, then the flat of the bay, the huddled houses, and all around them the vast, cloudless sky, bleached and empty save the sun's burning eye. And they felt invisible planes roaring through them, and even in this heat, they shivered.

Abrázame

The Mayhem Seat of the Church of Panic is located in a small, dark office space on 103rd and Lexington, above a Chinese restaurant, next to the El Barrio Associated and its De La Vega graffito. Trios of the faithful float in and out of there all day, they pass the boys on the corner who squint at them and make sly jokes when they alight the hill, heading south past the defunct El Tepeyak Records and the deli owners protected by Plexiglas, past the Pentecostal church at the top, where the parishioners have thrown open the doors and the percussion-thick Afropop gospel bobs heads across the street.

Lucas is in the Santa Rosa Taquería at the bottom of the hill. They have telenovelas on over the grill, bachata sneaking out of the jukebox, a man's voice, high and light and desperate with longing. The lyrics were a ballad once, backed by rock band and orchestra, but they have bootlegged and stolen their way across the music of Mexico, Colombia, the Dominican Republic, through salsa and merengue, to land here, in this place, among dried peppers and steam from the subway. The lyrics speak of love, love like nails in the stomach, like bullets passing through the brain. They speak with a directness that English fears, and they pull tears from the girl making tortillas in the kitchen because she is fifteen and sensitive; but Lucas cannot understand them.

Joaquín, Santa Rosa's owner, got his citizenship and bargained a huge debt on the success of this restaurant, and he has been winning. When they opened, it was three tables, paper plates, it was plastic utensils and drinking out of the bottle. He and his family gritted their teeth and spat. They bought the alley space next to the restaurant, put in five more tables, a bathroom, the jukebox. They bought thick plastic plates and glasses, got their liquor license, and at long last, people are coming in a steady trickle, the neighborhood business owners for lunch, construction workers, a few stray gringos with greasy hair and glasses, and now Joaquín is thinking about curtains and tablecloths. Just before closing, a friend from Oaxaca comes in with a bottle of tequila and they each nurse a straight shot while Joaquín does the books and the friend talks about his girlfriends. Sometimes he cries. I chase María but she never chases me. Coming here, opening your own place, using a calculator, Joaquín, you are the story of America. Joaquín frowns. It's not a story, he says. It's hard work.

"I don't understand them," Joaquín says to Lucas, waving his hand toward the Mayhem Seat. "Where is their god?

La Iglesia Pentecostal, I do not go to church but I know where their god is. The Church of Panic? What do they believe?"

"They are preparing for the Day, like the Pentecostals."

Joaquín shrugs. He can't read Lucas, doesn't want to offend him. He goes diplomatic. "Don Arroyo waited also, for years, to court my mother. He wrote a waltz and hired *músicos* to play it on the street below her window, spent months writing words to it that satisfied him, took lessons to learn how to sing it. He waited. He paced, around and around. At last, one August night, when he knew she was home, he brought the band over. On the last three notes, his voice broke, and she opened the window. My father was already there with her. Don Arroyo was confused. How did you win her? he said. And my father said, I saw her in the butcher and asked."

"You don't have to worry about offending me," Lucas says.

"A customer is a customer," Joaquín says.

The stairway to the Mayhem Seat is narrow and crooked, red walls below a musty skylight. On the door, they've painted an exclamation point, bold and square, engulfed in stylized red and yellow flames.

"Can I help you?" The man who answers the door looks Lucas over. Lucas's aura throws him off at first but he can smell the skepticism.

"I come as a seeker," Lucas says.

"Have you come to be saved?"

"Yes."

"Saved from what?"

Lucas hesitates, and then thinks of it: he extends his finger and points it with purpose at the ceiling, at the stark sky, at a planet, purple and blue, swaying around a double sun.

The man checks his watch, produces a compass, does some quick figures on a graphing calculator.

"Wrong," he says, and closes the door.

 Orphans

Wendell wakes in a hammock, rocking on the breeze of an air shaft. Around him, yellow orbs, spidery ladders; Piazzolla's bandoneón, accompanied by lush orchestra, strains through a radio. There is laughter, kind voices speaking in foreign tongues. The air is warm and soft and smells of sweet vegetables, a woman cooking peppers over a slow flame. All is well, everything says. This is a safe place. There is a bandage on his head from where the mug hit him—ah, he remembers now the fall, the black water—but his limbs are rejuvenated, as if he has slept for days, though he knows he hasn't: his insomnia cured him of that.

Masoud is next to him with a bottle of Red Stripe sweating half-empty in his hand, his feet up on a stack of pallets, toe tapping inside his shoe to the music. He smiles.

"Ah. Awake."

Wendell blinks. "Where are my glasses?"

"Here. Amazing that you did not lose them." He reaches over, puts them on Wendell's face. "They were worried about you."

"Because of the bottle."

"No. Because of the water. Nobody goes in there, they say. I hope you did not swallow so much of it."

He did, and the stuff is still coating his throat. Seven different strains of mutated bacteria will start a war for hegemony of his esophagus that will last for forty-six years. The victor, alone at last, will spread in triumph, and Wendell will develop a nagging cough in his seventies that will persist until death. In this, as in all things, Wendell is a lucky man. Another bacterium, unfettered, would have clogged his throat until it was hard to swallow, hard to breathe; another would have prepared his esophagial lining for cancer.

"Where are the Marsupials?"

"I do not know. We pulled you into the boat and left. You should have seen it. The whole subway car was swaying. Jets of green coming out of the windows. People falling into the water. Already I have said this, but I am amazed you are not hurt."

". . ."

"I was very worried about you."

"Are *you* all right?" Wendell says.

"Oh yes, yes. But I do not know about many of the people in the car. . . . Wendell, I am sorry. If I knew the Marsupials were crazy, I would never have . . . I did not know."

"I know that. I know. I just don't know where to go from here. We're hanging by a steel cable in a secret city, a mile below the people we know. My house is gone. And I still don't know where my baby is."

"We can start asking again—"

"—Ask? And bring those four maniacs down on us again? Masoud, they knew we were going there before we did. We're their prey."

"Then we will find another way. If Manuel is walking on this earth, my friend, we will find him." He drinks some more Red Stripe and smiles, but he can see Wendell is not convinced.

They have fallen in with the Ciphers, a group of immigrants in Under Tryon who live in a suspended tugboat. The rumors say most of them are Tajiks and Angolans with a small clan of Bolivians scattered among them. They sleep in quadruple-decker bunks and eat together from vats of spicy gumbo from the tug's boiler room, converted into a galley. To name themselves, they take the monikers of American and British rock stars and add a number; they speak to each other in a patois of Chinese, English, and Portuguese, words hung together in rough rhythm, meanings focused with exaggerated facial expressions, hand gestures. They look like vaudeville actors who've lost their top hats and canes. They started a business making firecrackers for the street dealers in Chinatown, big mothers that arc high above the city and explode into blooms that cover blocks, hordes of tiny ones that scramble and crackle like cockroaches. But the real money is in distribution, they've made a name moving things all around Darktown and the city above, car components, furniture, electrical equipment, guns, food, scrap metal. Local only. They have a few offices topside now, one in the 20s over an Indian restaurant, another in Long Island City next to the splay of overpasses flung off the Queensboro Bridge that dive into the neighborhood below. And one by one they are preparing to go, to return to the sun, shedding their numerical names and putting on another one, a first name, a last name, the same middle name to show they are all family, fighting to the surface arm in arm.

Ringo 5 brings Wendell a bottle of ginger ale; he lifts the bandage, presses two tender fingers around the wound.

"You are the one looking for Manuel," he says. "Oh, don't worry. I have no plans to reveal you. Why would I want your blood on my hands?"

"Money?"

Ringo 5 laughs. "We're interested in legitimate business here. Long-term growth. We like to joke that we'll know success is ours when we start paying taxes."

"Maybe you're like the Marsupials."

Masoud makes a noise, but Ringo 5 restrains him.

"I understand that the last few days have been unkind to you. But do not reject our hospitality. Your name and face are liabilities to you. We can show you how to change them. Show you how to speak a new tongue, as if you are a man astounded by every word, as if every complete sentence is a triumph—do not interrupt me, there is more. The man you are looking for does not want to be found. You will get no closer to him by asking, and posing the question enough times will kill you. Therefore, you must change from the man who asks to the man who seeks."

Ringo 5 reaches back, takes a sip of Masoud's beer. "Before you came down here, my friend, you were a cell in the bloodstream of this city. You flowed where the heart pushed you, you did not even see the walls of the arteries and veins that hemmed you in. The disappearance, the explosions, they were ruptures that cast you out and closed behind you. They have been bound up by police tape and newspaper. You are out of circulation now, and the rules have changed. No force propels you now, no direction is laid out for you, and if you are to find your way you must carve it out of the flesh of this world, write your false name on the wall wherever you go. Does your head feel better now?"

". . . what? Oh, yes."

"Good, because I have not finished yet. Mr. Apogee, do you love Manuel González?"

Yes yes yes yes yes.

"Because to find him, you must separate yourself forever from the people you know. Your identifiable corpse must be found by the proper authorities. Your coworkers must receive phone calls from the police. Word must pass among your friends that you have gone. Your parents, Mr. Apogee, must suffer the singular anguish of outliving their child. All that you have built on the surface, it must be as if you have cremated it and scattered the ash from a bluff. It must be the end of you, and to begin again is a fight. The Ciphers did it because we had nothing, we were orphans. To do it for love, when you have so much, is an act of consuming desperation."

Wendell Apogee thinks of Masoud, arms around him, saying get down, get down, charred paper raining in the street. He thinks of his father in his silver spacesuit, saluting to a

Polaroid camera. His mother disconnected the phone, welded the mailbox shut, covered the windows with garbage bags. They brought her out on a stretcher. Leave me, she said. You are motherless now. I can't lose you if you're already gone. He thinks of $576 rustling in his shirt pocket, the hills peeling into old Appalachia, splintered farms and stark houses, gas stations of unpainted cinder blocks and white plastic radios squealing out fiddle music from the festival over the ridge, and him with a soggy road map, a chewed-up duffel bag, cold coffee in a Styrofoam cup.

There are his friends, the people he loves. There is the Groove Squad, who tried to warn him, they will kill themselves with guilt imagining that there was something they could have done. For a few days it will seem inappropriate to play. There are Diane and the Ecuadorians; and Robert Lord Townsend, Jr., who introduced him to Manuel; and Lucas, who nursed Wendell one night when he was sick with love and alcohol, throwing up on his clothes, his longing turning his brain to babble. These people, who would open their arms to him if he arrived at their doors, greasy clothes and singed hair and all, they would still take him.

It is better to settle, Masoud had said. Better to return to his desk at work tomorrow in borrowed clothes, groggy on the telephone, waking from this as from a fever dream. Better to go back to eating in chili-lit Indian restaurants with sitar and tabla players in the window, drinking thick Turkish coffee with Daoud and letting Daoud tell him he's better off this way. He could find another man, sweet and kind;

they could retire to a house upstate with flowing windows, where the roads are framed in green and there are only the assured rhythms of farm equipment, occasional guests, the piling and melting of snow, mud in the spring, angry summers mollified by shade and wind. He could let this rage cut wrinkles into him and then dissipate. He could let solace in.

But he is here now. Subways mumble above his head, the tugboat shudders on its cables. Children swing from spindly walkways, singing songs over the thrum of music and machinery. Every second is another escape from death: it swings by, brushes your clothes, and then wheels around, cheated and livid, and you plant your feet on the crumbling rock, curl your hands into fists. Come and get me.

Burn yourself down and start over, Lucas would say. It's not so hard, the Ecuadorians would say. We did it. The Groove Squad would play again after only a few days. And here is Masoud, with expectant eyes that turn to the lattice of suspended houses outside the porthole, to the skiffs streaming below.

"I am already illegal," he says. "Masoud is my father's name."

Wendell sits up in bed and closes his eyes; around him are the chitters of salsa, the quick beats of hip-hop, the purr of boats rising and falling, the rattle and grumble of traffic as trains rise and fall, laced by one hundred sixty-seven languages, cut across by footsteps and the clank of hammers and stoves, counting off threes, counting off fives, and he could swear that in this minute, all these sounds are coming together, unifying to anticipate a massive One rushing up from the core of the earth, tearing down from the sky. Sixty-six. Sixty-five.

"What do I have to do?" he says.

 Smoke and Mirrors

By the time he was fifteen, Jimi 64 was kidnapped from a refugee camp and forced to fight on both sides of the Angolan civil war. He was shot four times and killed twenty-five men, eighteen with a thirty-year-old Russian machine gun, five more with a bayonet, another by holding his head under the water of a latrine. The last one he bludgeoned with a stone. Then a year of starving in the country, another as a prostitute in the demolished cities combed by marauders and strewn with corpses. He is the first to laugh at the thought that he survived all of that, and all that followed, only to be killed by influenza.

Jimi resembles Wendell in height and build. May we use your body after you're done with it, Ringo 5 asks. Of course, Jimi 64 says. It will be no good to me; and he smiles with a blear in his eye that shows already he is moving on. For the witnesses to Jimi 64's death, it appears painful. He is wracked by disfiguring coughs, spits up blood-striped phlegm before one final shudder. But Jimi, well, Jimi is beyond that. He is eighteen again and back on the slave ship, a dilapidated tanker, the hold stacked twenty layers high with wooden bunks on chains, swaying in a storm off Benguela. The slavers are climbing from bunk to bunk with cattle prods and pistols, they're shocking anyone who looks hostile and they've already shot six suspected organizers, but even these measures are far too late: on a signal from below, the slaves rise up and overwhelm their captors and drag them to the oily floor of the hold to break their necks and dismember them, the metal walls vibrate with the mutineers' triumphant hollers, and Jimi 64 stumbles to the deck in a pelting rain and laughs, for the ship is turning with purpose toward the Western Hemisphere, and he knows at long last he is free, the manacles are coming off, the bonds on his ankles will be sawed away, and he will follow the path of birds, across the ocean, over the sea.

They send the body to Professor Sturgeon, a disgraced plastic surgeon and model ship builder who alters Jimi 64's teeth to match Wendell's dental records, puts him in Wendell's clothes, and brings him to the surface. By rowboat he conveys Jimi 64 to a strait of water between Manhattan and Roosevelt Island. The cable car lurches overhead, huge freighters threaten to eat the little craft, but Sturgeon remains calm. He observes the pattern of the current, the movement of tides, balances the combination of weights that will let the body float below the draft of the freighters for three weeks, food for hagfish, until the body snags in a pier not far from the first body found in the Financial District. So Jimi 64 makes his way to the slab of Dr. Gore, who sees obvious discrepancies, something about the bones that's not quite right. She has Wendell's prints from the police files of Pilot Mountain, North Carolina, a fight he'd been in down there, a night in jail. She wishes she had a DNA sample from Wendell to match the John Doe, wishes the John

Doe had fingertips to match to Wendell's. But she has neither of these things, and the teeth are a perfect match, so she starts making phone calls.

The remains are cremated; a service is held in the Catholic church close to Wendell's apartment, though most of his friends are sure he was not raised in that faith. The priest is generous, his sermon is good considering he had never met the deceased in his life. Though a quiet and reserved man, the priest says, Wendell had a fire in him, a passion. The tragedy is that his life was too short to let him share it with the world.

They are all there. Robert Lord Townsend, Jr. is in an angular suit, a tie with a gold pin, Ma Xiao Ling in a black jacket, the Ecuadorians in deepening shades of gray. Lucas staggers in after the urn has been conducted to the altar; it looks like he's just woken up, he rubs his eyes with his thumbs and sits next to Diane, in front of the entire Groove Squad, who stand in a long row, hands clasped in front of them, heads bowed. They sing the hymns in a syncopated five-part harmony that sets the stained glass to humming.

"Disappearances and funerals, that's all we're good at," Ma Xiao Ling says later. "Why can't anyone get married?"

"Did you know they're thinking of putting in a monorail from Red Hook to lower Manhattan?" Sylvia says. "Right over the water, they say they'll add the other rail if enough people actually use it. . . ."

"Here try some of this, it'll knock your socks off," Izzy says.

"And the octopus says—" The Slug says.

"—It was suicide, wasn't it?" Robert Lord Townsend, Jr. says.

They are eating in an Italian restaurant across the street from the church, they've gone through the first bottles of wine and it seemed as though the party was about to start, but at this they all set their forks down; the punch line across the table fails, they eat laughter.

"Wasn't it?" he continues. "A man doesn't just find his way into the East River."

"The Queensboro Bridge," someone says.

"Or the Triborough. It could have been the Triborough." It is so easy to imagine: Wendell on the bridge, leaning against the fence; nobody sees him as he climbs over. It is not dramatic. He does not hang white-knuckled from the edge first, plagued by the desire to live; no, he just lets himself over and falls without screaming into the dark water, and then the bricks sewn into his clothes pull him down. The great foundations of the bridge soaring above are like the ruins of Egyptian temples flooded by the Aswan Dam. Ships two hundred years old tap against them, they hold species of fish uneaten by man. Over his head, a freighter churns the water, he can see the huge object slipping over him, screws turning chaos in their wake, whirlpools within whirlpools, collapsing and exploding in and out of each other, and then that last bit of oxygen is used, the heart turns over one last time, the brain relaxes, says good night, everyone. Good night.

"It wasn't a suicide, though," one of the Groove Squad says, then swallows his chicken. "Friends. Brothers. That is a fiction."

"You think someone killed him?" Diane says.

"I don't think the man is dead."

Ma Xiao Ling leaves the funeral party alone, clicks in sharp heels toward the subway. She is two blocks away before Robert Lord Townsend notices she's gone, and she's covered another block before he catches up, a blister already rising on his toe from his hard shoes. She turns to find him panting, wiping his mouth, trying to speak, lines of sweat forming on his suit.

"You don't run much," she says.

"No. I never have taken to it. Even when I was a boy. I was the one on the playground in the little suit, walking from swing to swing, wondering why everyone was in such a rush."

"You could afford it."

"That's true."

"So why are you running today?"

He strains to smile, but his hands shake; she can see his cleverness leaving him, pooling around his feet, melting into the sidewalk. How much he must want her, she thinks, that all those years of schooling cannot give him the words.

"It's only death," she says. "Don't let it make you say something stupid."

". . ."

". . ."

"The Slug's having a party this weekend," he says. "I hope you're going."

"Maybe I will," she says.

She does not. Nine years later, she will drive across the ravaged plains to California, eight generators and a box full of parts rattling behind her, only at night with the headlights off, praying not to meet a deer, a child, an abandoned car wreck. During the day, she will hide the truck in a barn, a drainage ditch, the ruin of a house, crawl underneath it and try to sleep. It is no worse than the Yangtze, she will think, when the bullets were coming for her; it is no worse than the smuggler's cargo plane, where icicles grew on their hands and they threw the corpses into the atmosphere over the Pacific. Now, dirt in her mouth, hiding in water and machinery. She will know she has no choice but to accept the changes, will come to understand her time in New York as a respite from that, a few small years of peace, and she will be glad she did not fool herself then into thinking it would last, only get better. All things come and go, people come and go; and there, under a truck beneath a pulsing gray sky, she will wonder what became of Robert Lord Townsend, regret that she did not go to that party, balance herself on tiptoes, and kiss him when she had the chance.

Two bouts with malaria, a gunshot wound, lone survival of a plane crash, and seven years later, she will have the chance again, at a gas station half-buried in the sand of the Arizona desert. She will be trading forty-six yards of PVC piping for three gallons of petroleum. He will be leaning against a rusted phone booth, smoking, pretending to ignore the owner's warnings to put it out. In the dark, the dust, the change the years have wrought, they will almost not recognize each other. Then the cigarette will fall from his fingers, the gasoline spill across the pavement, as they run toward each other, their laughter making idiots of them both.

The Numbers Don't Lie

Diane walks the mile under the expressway by the tire repair shops and housing projects to reach the stretch of warehouses along Columbia, the soggy tenement on Van Brunt where Lucas lives. The funeral was the first time she'd seen him since Manuel disappeared, and the change in him unsettled her. Bedraggled, unshaven. Eyes bleary. Signs that the self-discipline, the rigor, were slipping.

He buzzes her into the building without checking to see who it is. He does not call down from the window. The door to his apartment throws a blade of light across the hallway, and judging from the plates of food piled there, it's possible that it has been open for days. Inside, the floor of the apartment is covered with huge charts, maps, diagrams, circles drawn around clusters of numbers, notes etched beside them in Lucas's architectural handwriting. Arrows drawn in red, pointing to other charts. And Lucas squats in the middle of this in his underwear, six different pens in his hand, his head twitching from one picture to another, talking to itself.

"Lucas?"

"—What?"

"You look like shit."

"Always the raconteur. Though I prefer it to politeness, which wastes the precious hours we have on this earth."

"What are you doing?"

He gazes at the atlas of lines and shapes around him. "I have no time to explain."

"Fucking explain."

"Why do you always resort to profanity?"

"I'm not leaving until you tell me what you're doing."

He makes a notation.

"Lucas."

"Fine. Fine. I have been looking into the activities of the Church of Panic. I attempted, of course, to procure this information in a simple and direct manner, but the followers of the Church did not allow it. So I had to adopt more subversive measures. What you are looking at here...no, here...are a set of documents carried, it appears, by one member of each triad of the Church. Do you know what these are?"

"Why would I know?"

"Good question. I did not know myself until a few days ago. But then I saw here...well, wait a moment. I have to take a few steps back. Do you know what the Church is? What it values?"

"Um..."

"It is an apocalyptic religious organization that believes that the end of civilization is coming through some kind of...event in the sky. Of course, everything else follows: days and nights of unending darkness, oceans rising to swallow the land. The particular recipe of mayhem and destruction is incidental here. There is little in the belief system of the Church of Panic, at least in its archetype, that differs from any other style of Western religious mania. What is different is all of the data I have on my floor here."

"Which shows what?"

"Proof. In one sense, Miss Prom Queen, the Church of Panic is not religious at all, because they have proof that the end is near. This information here, it is the wound in Christ's side, presented to us for examination. It is the stigmata for us to put our hands in and explore."

"I don't follow you."

"Something is coming, Diane. Something is approaching our planet at an alarming rate."

"Something like the moon?"

"You see now why I did not want to explain this to you. You think I am relapsing, that the effects of the deprogramming have worn off, or some other such psychological voodoo. You think I am reverting to a faith that even in my childhood I could not bring myself to believe."

"Aren't you?"

"Look at the signs! The things that keep appearing over this city that we read about in the paper and can't explain. Look at the data. It all suggests one unavoidable conclusion: that the end is here . . . finally here. . . ."

"Listen to yourself, Lucas. Look at the way you look. Where did you get all of this, anyway?" She waves at the papers on the floor.

"I stole it, from one of the churchgoers."

"What do you mean, 'stole'? You didn't mug them, did you?"

". . ."

"You mugged them, Lucas! Jesus!"

"I had to see this for myself."

"That's it, I'm going—"

"No. Stay. Let me explain myself to you."

"I don't want to hear it."

She turns to go, then stops. "Lucas Henderson, you are not allowed to go insane on me. I love you too much." And with that, she leaves him, his hair standing in angles and, for the first time in many years, his tongue struck dumb. He thinks of Diane later when he is on the train moving north, back up to Spanish Harlem. But she is out of his head when he mounts the dark stairs again, stands before the Church of Panic's door. The exclamation point on fire.

"Can I help you?"

"Yes. I want to join your church."

"You can't."

"But I have to. I have seen the numbers, I have seen the movement in the air. I look at these millions of people in the street who are always looking forward, or looking to the side, or they have their faces in phones or magazines. I want to raise my arm and point at the sun, and I want all those heads to wake up, turn upward, and see. Something is coming, and we are not prepared. Do not shut me out of this. It is too much to bear."

The man looks at the two robed figures behind him. All three nod in unison.

"Welcome to the Church, friend."

CHAPTER 5

In Which Many Things Change

 Deserters

It is cooler today; life grows in the neighborhood. The old Dominicans, the ones who were middle-aged before the crack
wars, sit in plastic lawn chairs on the sidewalk. They drink
beers from a stained Playmate cooler and argue about politics
in Santo Domingo from forty years ago. The young ones
stand near the walls of the parks, smile and call each other
motherfucker, their arms around each other's shoulders. Cars
pass with windows open, shaking merengue, and they whistle
to the people in the apartments. For the first time in weeks,

nobody is sweating through his clothes, nobody mops his brow. It is a good day, the best day of the year, people will say. Tomorrow we'll be sweating like your mother in heat.

Inside his dark room, El Flaco sits in his wool suit and smokes. He is confused. It does not bother him that fewer people want to be smuggled into the country. The roilings of war, disease, financial collapse are fickle. For three months, he may be overwhelmed with refugees, people so desperate that they are willing to spend three weeks sealed in an oil barrel or locked in the trunk of a car just to get to the slums of this country. Then in the next three months, just a few stray political dissidents, here and there a deposed government official, name changed, skin pigment altered. This is normal. What confuses him today is that, for the first time in seventeen years, people have come to him asking to be smuggled *out*. I want to be back in Guatemala by the end of this week. How can I get into Uzbekistan tomorrow without being detected? They get their counterfeit passports and buy tickets for Brazil, they book flights in the tiny planes that get them halfway to places in the Amazon where people do not live. They go to Indonesia. There are islands that are still uninhabited, they say. The old-timers, the ones who were smuggling people into the United States before El Flaco was born, say there were evacuations like that during the Cuban Missile Crisis; before that, a few Germans during World War Two, Japanese fleeing the internment camps. But this is bigger than any of those. What are you running from? El Flaco asks them, folding the bills in half with his fingers and sliding them into his pocket. They do not answer him. They say: there's another hundred for you if you can get me out by tomorrow.

All of the immigrants seem to know about it. They talk about it in their cramped apartments crowded with bunk beds, in the rows of telephone booths in the check-cashing stores, in the backs of trucks rattling out to Long Island to work construction. It is a flood of information passing from family to family. Something big is going to go down, and the immigrants are deserting, they're abandoning ship. In the neighborhoods of the outer orbit of success, people are stock-piling food, they're buying gallons of water, firearms. Their employers catch little of this, it does not reach the ears of reporters, bankers, stockbrokers, or restaurant owners, no. In the neighborhoods near the burning center, magazine editors and software designers are going to lunch, foundation officers and academics meet in carpeted offices with panoramic views of the jagged cityscape, financial consultants make phone calls to venture capitalists, day traders flash signals to each other in noisy stockmarkets. They worry about buying good wine, business deals, replacing buzzing refrigerators, weekend entertainment. They jockey for jobs, think about buying cars, wonder if their spouses are cheating on them. They have no idea.

El Flaco pulls the heavy curtain open. He can see down the wide valley of Broadway, and the sounds rise up to him as a clanking, orchestral din. At least three quarters of them must know the news, El Flaco thinks. How many of them are preparing to leave? And is my Lavinia among them?

Our Hero, Part 2

The Ciphers are gathered on the deck of the tugboat around a long table set with chipped china, twisted silverware. On the corner of the deck, a mariachi band waits, the horn players blow the spit from their instruments, press their lips against the mouthpieces. The guitar player checks his tuning again and again, killing time. Around them all, a web of light, colored bulbs, Christmas twinklers, tiki lamps, candles shivering in hurricane lanterns.

"What name has he chosen?" Sid 79 says.

"I heard Tom Jones. Odysseus Candide."

"Odysseus Candide? A little pompous, isn't it?"

"For a few days, it was Jonny Quest."

"Better."

Sid 79's father was a prizefighter in Kyrgyzstan, taught him at the age of seven what he knew about how to hurt men. Sid 79 began fighting three years later, kept losing because of his small size, compensated for it by making a deal with a Chinese dissident in hiding, trading martial arts lessons for protection from the secret service. At fifteen he began winning matches, making money. He fought his way out of Central Asia, through the Balkans, fought his way onto a ship bound for the United States, fought even with six gang boys in Bridgeport who tried to steal his hat; he left them lying on the sidewalk in front of a Mexican deli while he took the train to New York with commuters who would never have guessed how many bones his hands had broken.

The walls of the tug's hold were lined with weapons: swords, buck knives, shuriken, assegais. In panels in the floor, machine guns, mortars, and rocket launchers, the remnants of the Ciphers' revolutionary days. All these things will be your friends, Sid 79 said. When Wendell tried to touch them, Sid 79 knocked him down and kicked him in the stomach.

"Not yet," said Sid 79.

There is a shout from below, and the band begins to play, an uptempo oom-pah that reminds everyone of how polka sneaked into Mexico.

"His hand-to-hand skills were abysmal at first."

"What did you expect?"

"Not abysmal. Though his marksmanship compensated. Tin cans at seventy-five yards, rifle, pistol, or crossbow."

"Crossbow?"

"He wanted a gimmick."

Wendell flailed at Sid 79 with a two-by-four while Sid parried with an assegai. Wendell swung wide, and Sid 79 hurled the assegai through the crotch of Wendell's pants, pinned him to the wall.

"You're not ready," he said.

Wendell's arms screamed with the strain of pulling back the arrow, the string bit his arm with the snap of release. He did a handspring, a backflip. He approached Sid 79 with a short knife; Sid 79 engaged with bare hands. For four seconds it was acrobatic, they leapt around each other, spinning in the air, but then Wendell was on the floor, Sid 79's left foot across his throat.

"You're going to kill me," Wendell said.

Sid 79 smiled. "Are you kidding? You're the best student I've had in years."

Ringo 5 and Sid 79 emerge from the hold first, beaming for the weakling who became their star pupil. Masoud follows; he has become leaner, his arms and legs show definition, he has not been in this kind of shape since his fighter pilot days, running across burning sand, chasing girls in Beirut and Damascus, trying to bury his brother. And at last, the man of honor steps onto the deck. At first they do not recognize him. The weight he has lost makes him look taller; his head is now bald, he has a pointed mustache, a devilish beard, his glasses tinted a deep purple. He is dressed in the loose-fitting clothes of an immigrant, save the light green Converse hi-tops and a long red scarf that floats behind him on the air, like an aviator; his weapons glare across his back.

"I saw you train today," Masoud said. "Did you really beat Sid 79 with the quarterstaffs?"

"I think he let me," Wendell said.

"I do not think that man would let anyone beat him."

Wendell contemplates this.

"So what will you do now?"

"It seems there are only four people in this entire city who know where Manuel might be."

"They will not talk to you."

"I don't intend to talk to them."

The music quickens, the Ciphers stand and explode with

applause, for the person that came to them was only a man, but he is a comic book hero now, something archetypal. The Man Who Seeks.

"Go forth and find what you are looking for—" Ringo 5 cocks an eyebrow. "—Captain Spaceman."

That was for you, Dad.

Love and Illicit Trade

The news flies from the tugboat, streaks out across cables, on the rocking rafts, in the oily air. They are talking about it on the docks, Darktown Market throngs with a stew of information and gossip; it is the topic of bars and the conversation around portable generators, the speech of middlemen waiting for shipments. The smugglers won't talk about anything else. The rumors say the Spaceman is bionic, that he is made of titanium; they say he has extra appendages hidden under his clothing, his glasses conceal mechanical eyes that allow him to see infrared light and throw out ropes of electricity. How could they not, they say. How could he beat the Horsemen otherwise? This is the only fact about Captain Spaceman that the storytellers of Darktown do not change, because it is so foolhardy, so brave and stupid: Captain Spaceman is looking for the Four Horsemen, to challenge and best them in single combat.

The four giants in raincoats earned this moniker after their attack on Hyrvygeena; they were so savage, seemed so invincible. Everyone who was there has a story, of climbing out of the bar and plummeting into the water, leaping to another house, climbing chains arm over arm. They remember the subway car sliced open by fire, and the ones who were hiding close by saw what happened to the Marsupials. They refused to give up, even after the Horsemen lost interest in them. Asshole was the last to go, dragging the bones of his legs across the floor after the flesh had been burnt off them, issuing insults until they all turned on him at once to silence him. They held a service for them in an evangelical chapel shaped from an old Greyhound bus: they played their album, those who had experienced them described what crazy bastards they were, and they were committed to memory, there being no solid remains to care for. But the Horsemen remain, a malevolent force in the underground city. They came looking for González, for Apogee, but now they seem to kill at random: men and women in the market, on boats, in their homes. Death by green fire, screaming, hands on their faces or swarming in the air in front of them, as if to bat away the flames. Their neighbors talk about the stench that follows; contrary to Darktown custom, nobody occupies their abandoned houses, for the superstition is too great about those places. The vigilante squads are trying to understand how the deaths are linked, what the Horsemen are here for, but the connections between the dead, between the dead and still living, are too vast. Love and illicit trade, kinship, sponsorship. Sworn enemies. Doctor and patient. A web of favors, money laundering. But one man stands in the calm eye of this hurricane: guess who.

It was his trafficking, they say, the people he was willing to screw over; no, no, it is the anger of a thousand jilted lovers personified. No, the old ones say: it is Manuel's sorcery that brought the Horsemen down on us. He could do hexes, he knew the signs, he made the sacrifices, but he was ever careless with his art; and we are the victims of his recklessness.

It is like an old Western now when the Horsemen appear. People dive under tables, they jump out of windows into the water, they stutter, force a laugh, then dash for the door. And wherever Captain Spaceman goes, the din of Darktown is quelled, people look him over in silence. They are checking his costume for salvageable valuables. They just want to see the man. They are appraising his skills in the way he walks, the tone of his muscles. The bookies in the rooms built under a foundation of the BQE have started a fierce betting pool on the coming fight, 7–3 for the Horsemen, 37–1 for the Spaceman and his sidekick. The big money is on the Horsemen; Dr. Ease and a collection of Spaniards have put down thirty thousand apiece and are already spending like they've won the seventy. But people are betting on the underdog, too: the recent immigrants who are too in debt to leave are putting twenty-five, fifty dollars on it, their last shot home. El Flaco has three hundred. The boaters' guild collected fourteen hundred fifty. The risk is acceptable, they say, for that big payoff; and besides, they see something in him. The boys of Hyrvygeena are his best men, they've got eighteen hundred together riding on him, and he and Masoud always get a seat when they come looking for information. Free drinks, too, though they never touch them.

"Has anyone spotted the Horsemen?" the Spaceman says.

"No," Hackerin' Pete says. "But you'll be the first to know if we hear anything. We'll find you. Just do me a favor"—and here he leans in close, his voice stifles a sob—"you get the sons of bitches that did this to my bar."

"We haven't seen them, Captain," they tell him at the market. "If they come this way, though, we'll use these." They hold up flare guns with Cyrillic characters on them. They're grinning.

An old man pulls him close. "You win that fight, dammit. I've got everything on you. If you lose, and they don't kill you, I'm going to find you and kill you myself."

He's their champion, their protector, their flying knight in hi-tops, crossed with quivers and pistols. They want to help him: they give him a roll call of the dead they can identify, search for the names that used to signify the piles of ash, splinters of bone, that the Horsemen leave behind. But it is not enough; no pattern emerges from the noise. Captain Spaceman perches in the bow of the Ciphers' tugboat, waiting for news, for messengers to come; but there are only the sounds of faraway music, the creak of houses swaying on cables, the grumble of trains above.

Masoud comes bearing coffee. Wendell refuses.

"If that is what you want . . . ," Masoud says. He sits along the railing. "How do you say it . . . a penny for your thinking?"

"Thoughts. For my thoughts."

"And do I in fact give you a penny, or do I only say it?"

"You just say it. The penny's implied."

". . ."

". . ."

"So . . . a penny for your thoughts?"

Wendell's back is to him, but Masoud can hear his mouth form a quick smile. Or frown.

"You are doubting that you have done the correct thing."

"No," Wendell says.

"You are afraid of the Horsemen."

"You know, I'm really not."

"That is a lie."

"No, it's not, it's . . . It's been, what, almost a month now, since he left. A month, and there's still this feeling, a thing in my chest stretched tight, tight enough to have a pitch, like it could break at any second. For the first few days I thought it would just snap in two. But it won't. It just stays there, thrumming, and I want so much for it to stop that I almost don't care anymore if it has to break to do it."

"But if it breaks, that will be worse, will it not?"

"It'll be a change."

"But you are talking about your heart."

". . ."

"When my father died," Masoud says, "my brothers and I, we did not know what to do. My mother had died many years before that, giving birth to my third brother. This when I was five, and it is very difficult for me even to remember her. My father was family. He was father and mother and uncle and grandmother. We scattered across the world when he died, my brothers and I. One became a smuggler. One joined the Lebanese army, became an expert at defusing bombs. I became a fighter pilot. We had an anger in us and we believed we had to spend it, we had to hand it back to the world. One brother did not survive it. The other struggles with it still. He has a wife, a small boy, but a part of him cannot wait to die. I understand this feeling. I used to have it myself. But I remember, in a flight over Syria, I realized in one moment that I was too tired to fight like that anymore. Now, we are like an old married couple, my anger and I. We fight, and sometimes we do not speak to each other. But I know it is not going to leave me, and, Wendell, I do not want it to go. We are, how do you say it? We are settling."

His speech is dragging him too close to the place in his head where his brother stands in a linen suit, arms folded, frowning; and his voice breaks, his throat pinches, for a moment no words can come. He backs away, hands out, in accord with the truce he has made with the dead. His brother is willing to allow Masoud days, sometimes weeks, without reminding him of his betrayal, so long as Masoud does not attempt to resolve it, to organize his past into a fiction with an ending that claims it all happened to a younger man, in another country. It is acceptable this way. But sometimes it is very hard.

"It is not so bad to settle, my friend. It is a quiet life," Masoud says.

"You know I don't want to do that yet."

"Then you will stay as you are? I thought it was too much for you to bear."

"No, it's—"

"—No, listen to me. You cannot complain that it hurts and then not allow yourself the choice to settle. They are joined, these things. You love him too much for your heart not to break over it. Either give up the love or prepare for the break. That is the choice you have."

"What makes you think you know me so well?"

"I know you better than anyone now," Masoud says. "To half of the city, you are dead. To the other half, you have just been born. I am the only one that knows the truth."

"You're the only person I have left in this world," Wendell says.

"It is a good thing that I am staying then, eh?"

"Why are you staying, anyway?"

"To repay a debt. And because I have never met anyone quite like you."

"..."

"After we have found Manuel, we must return to the cockfight. It is unfair that you were not able to stay for the big matches at the end. Tens of thousands of dollars placed on every bird."

"Sounds familiar."

Masoud chuckles.

"This is going to kill us, isn't it," Wendell says.

"Maybe it will. Does that change your mind?"

"No."

Masoud smiles. "I did not expect it would."

 ## Schisms

Inspector Salmon finishes reading the autopsy report, clasps his hands. He gazes at the photos on the bulletin board. Another picture of Manuel, given to him by Lucas, this one taken not more than three weeks before he disappeared: he is smiling but looks haggard; he bears the lines of a man who does not sleep. He floats above the crowd around him. Here is one of Wendell, asleep on a pink and brown couch, facedown, mouth open, glasses pushed up on his face: a night that got out of hand, that he wakes from achy and sheepish, ready to apologize. One dead, one still missing, but Salmon expects that Manuel will turn up soon, he will surface in some body of water, or be found wedged into a Dumpster. Or a demolition crew will find him jumbled in an abandoned apartment when they inspect the building before they tear it down.

Salmon has already constructed a plot that satisfies him. In this story, Manuel wants to disappear, has to. He is pursued by assassins, hunted for bounty. It's possible, he was involved in so much: Salmon has never had a file so big on someone who appears nowhere on the public record. Or maybe he just wanted to go. He had to get out, he had to burn himself down and start over. And Wendell, out of desperate love, convinced Manuel to let him go too. So they went together, destroyed everything and left. But they didn't get far: Manuel's vanishing act was not complete, and they found him and shot him anyway; and Wendell in grief hurled himself into the water to drown. It's a good story, it explains all the information he has, and he believes now that if Manuel's body ever shows up, the autopsy will reveal wrongful, explainable death. Shooting, stabbing, poisoning. Maybe strangulation. And the strange corpse? Unrelated.

"I am not convinced," says Trout.

"We have Apogee's cadaver. What more do you need?"

"Dr. Gore herself raises significant doubts as to its identity."

"The dental records match."

"Anomalies remain. Dr. Gore said and I quote, one wishes we were in possession of material for a DNA sample of Mr. Apogee to corroborate the dental evidence, for even circumstantial evidence allows one to argue that the cadaver is in fact not that of Apogee unquote."

"Most of his friends think it was suicide."

"Some of them believe he is yet living."

"That's just denial."

"Perhaps. But we must try to keep an open mind."

"As long as we can close the case."

"Without evidence regarding the ultimate fate of Mr. González? I think not."

"Fine. Think not. Go on using that precious instinct of yours to make a fiction out of nothing."

Trout gives him a look, he is reminding him again, but Salmon puts up a hand to show that he's beginning to resent it. Yes: before Lucy Rutman, he thought like Trout did, he made leaps, drew connections between disparate elements of a case that seemed spurious but revealed themselves as pivotal. Salmon and Trout. The police put them on a case when all else had failed. They were the men who solved impossible crimes.

But Lucy's murder changed all that. Lucy, a woman who called the police when she learned someone was stalking her, leaving cryptic clues. Trout and Salmon's profile imagined the man as a delusional paranoid possessed of a vivid belief system involving a cult of machinery. They deduced that he reckoned time according to a binary calendar, an interlocking system of sixteen modulations of zeroes and ones; they predicted that the murder would take place in eighteen days, or on the day of sixteen ones. It happened eleven days early, and the murderer was not a machine enthusiast; it was her neighbor, a pet store owner who watched her with binoculars, knocked on her door, raped and killed her. A hideous, banal mix of frustration and attempts at control. Trout was saddened but unperturbed; but Salmon realized with horror that if the two of them hadn't made the story so damn complicated, they just might have saved Lucy's life. His methods of detection changed. He began to always look for the simple, the tight explanation that accounted for all they knew and nothing more. Solid detective work.

To Trout, this is a catastrophe. True, the change in Salmon still allows them to function as a team, but their ideas are formed now only through friction, they end with a solution that lies there, inert. Once, they were jazz musicians, riffing on each other's half-formed thoughts until they arrived through improvisation at a new place, in unfamiliar territory. They are opposites now, but once they were complements; they are partners now, but once they were friends, held together by bonds that did not require them to speak. Salmon's hand is still up, calling for quiet, because he can tell that Trout still wants to say something. So the second passes when Trout is allowed to say that he misses his fellow fish. How did our friendship falter? he wants to say; but the moment is gone.

"I do not think that we should close the case," Trout says.

"Why not."

"Because we should . . . at the very least, we should wait. If there are no more explosions, I will concede victory. But given the unusual nature of these conflagrations, and the strange corpse you are prepared to dismiss, we should allow for repeat performances."

And sure enough, it comes, this time on the Lower East Side. The victim is caught in the flames and scorched beyond recognition, is identified through DNA evidence and her impressive criminal record. Roselia Cruz: numerous convictions for drug smuggling, illegal shipping of hazardous chemicals. Each time, the sentence was stiff; each time, it was knocked down to something slight due to a hidden but irresistible influence on the justice system. In the last two years, also, it looks like she found religion, dropping through the strata of fundamentalist Christian faiths to land in a local cult.

"The Church of Panic," Trout says. "Its head office, which they have given the endearing name of the Mayhem Seat, is located—"

"—In Spanish Harlem. You've seen them, right?"

"Of course. You do not suppose a connection exists between deaths by strange fires and a cult whose members float a few inches off the ground?"

Salmon bristles. He is tired, he wants things to be simple. He wants a death, a cause; if there is a killer, a motive that humans can dream of. The drugs, the chemical trafficking, the enemies she must have made, these facts can explain everything, can't they? He looks at Manuel and Wendell on his board. Every day he tries to bury them, but they keep crawling out of their graves.

The man who answers the door at the Mayhem Seat could smell their skepticism a block away, two gringos *sin fe,* without any faith at all. He can smell their condescension now, the way Trout's abiding interest in religion is akin to his interest in the behavior of herd animals. Standing in front of him in their suits and flecked shoes, their godlessness is stifling.

"You are not welcome here," he says.

Trout sighs. "We are officers of the law, purveyors of justice. It matters little whether we are welcome or ... what are you doing?"

Behind the man at the door, several members of the church are floating around the office in a hurried fashion. They are taking diagrams off the walls, they are jamming books into boxes.

"Tell him," one of them says.

"Tell him nothing," says another.

"To maintain the surprise is to side with Them. We know that. Even the faithless must be admitted."

"No. No. We can't save them all. We can't even save our-selves."

"Do not start a second schism," says a third.

"Do we have any choice? Hunted down like rabbits, and we do nothing—"

"—Hey! Ixnay in front of the officersay. . . ."

"The Mayhem Seat is being dismantled," the man who answered the door says. "Do not try to find us."

"One question," Trout says, raising a finger. "Is the Seat an actual chair, or is it a metaphor like the county seat—" But the door is already closed.

Trout and Salmon look at each other.

"What was *that* about?" Salmon says.

 Speak Now

Robert Lord Townsend, Jr.'s great-grandfather, cursed with longevity, started the family fortune with real estate specula-tion in the West, moved into textiles before reproducing at the age of seventy-two with his fourth wife, the daughter of a coal miner who could not attend the wedding on account of black lung. His grandfather swelled the fortune during the world wars with munitions factories; then he married the daughter of an upstanding physician and stockholder, she herself no slouch at finance. His father, the first Robert Lord Townsend, turned his great wealth to pharmaceuticals, married the daughter of a Greek aristocrat. The fortune is made now, its tremendous bulk spread through hundreds of assets; generations of Townsends will have to employ immense creativity to squander it all. Robert Lord Townsend, Jr., has hatched several schemes to do just that, but prefers not to follow through on them. Why should he, when he can do nothing? Ah, but there are the board meetings: chicken-necked men in brown suits, jowls rustling, a nervous accountant with a yellowed collar describing benchmarks, and, when they meet at Townsend Enterprises, Inc., an oil painting of the first Townsend over the table, a lanky man in coat and tails whose name appears on the plate as Peter Holmes Townsend, but who Robert knows was in fact called Hell. Hell Townsend, who would have used the coat and tails to tourniquet gunshot wounds. A man who carried eight pistols on his person at all times, who disemboweled three men with a carriage axle and bribed the judge at his trial in Los Angeles, back when the city was a dustball gasping on the shores of the Pacific. Hell Townsend was a motherfucker. Robert sometimes imagines him materializing on the boardroom table, and oh, the havoc he wreaks. It always ends with the table on fire, the board members running for their lives, and Hell digging his fingers into the ceiling, knocking holes in the wall and howling. Men like that are the ones who make fortunes. The rest of us are just pushing numbers around.

But they are not at Townsend Enterprises, Inc., today; they are in the glass saucer perched atop the building that houses the offices of Hauser Pharmaceuticals International, which bears a complicated relationship to Townsend Enterprises that Robert knows is important, but does not bother to understand.

"... so as you can see from ah, from thirty-seven bee, earnings have ah exceeded benchmarks by point oh two percent for this quarter, a, ah promising lead-in to the next quarter ..."

The view from the saucer is spectacular: the buildings of the Financial District rising in clusters all around them like quartz crystals, the geode of Midtown spiking up farther away, the Empire State Building jutting, improbable, inescapable. Far below and away, the rooftops and water towers of the rest of the island shimmer, the piano key piers on the shore of Brooklyn, the drumming stretch of Queens. Crystal and music, he always thinks of the view in those terms, a deep hymn played on water glasses. From this vantage he imagines he could be Lord of the City, the man with the all-seeing eye, who beholds the movement of people across the surface as he sees storms approaching from the Jersey coast. Were he a tyrant, he could work great destruction from this height. But he would not. No, the Lord of the City would be generous and wise, slow to anger, fair in judgment. The millions of people below, tapping their feet at stoplights, opening and closing doors—was it true that if they all went out in the street at once they wouldn't fit?—would pay homage to him, they would raise their knishes and shawarma in his honor. He would try to meet each citizen of the metropolis in person, allow each one the chance to speak, let the words rise in wondrous cacophony, for didn't they all crave that chance, the voices of the living and the dead? To say something, to dig a groove in the record of the world? This is who I am. This is what I want.

And he would get his board members drunk. This last image remains with him on the ear-popping elevator ride to the street: these old men, necks wagging, legs reeling, their tongues loosened into hilarious vulgarity they will later deny, having the best time of their lives.

 Death Comes for Everyone

"Captain Spaceman . . . Captain Spaceman . . ."

The words scratch against the side of the tug, their speaker climbs around the outside of it. He knocks on a porthole, then his head snaps back to shoot a glance over his shoulder; he hides, but returns, knocks on another porthole, whispers again.

"Captain Spaceman, where are you? I need your help. . . ."

Wendell leans over from the bow. "Up here—"

"—*Shh!* The Horsemen can hear for miles. . . ."

The man, Boris Ilych Sestanovich, met Manuel three years ago, when Manuel was running a shipment of guns and machine parts out of Bulgaria. Sestanovich was small time then, very small time: cigarettes, some alcohol, a few prescription pharmaceuticals. They met in a nightclub in Burgas that played nothing but funk and soul; that night it was flipping through the pages of *Talking Book*, music that makes your hips move, that makes you think about love. They split a bottle of vodka, one of Sestanovich's better ones, and then Manuel had a proposition.

"I have no idea why he asked me," Sestanovich says. "He never gave me good reasons for anything."

It started as bank fraud, forging currency. He dealt with brokers, talented artists, a few men with split lips. Decent people. A lucrative trade. Manuel vanished for eight months, and Sestanovich bought a house in Slovenia overlooking the Danube for his new bride, a seamstress and soccer player. He and his wife fixed up his car, considered buying a boat to moor along the valley when they were in need of romance. The money kept coming; Sestanovich and his wife befriended one of the counterfeiters, a timid man who played a beautiful accordion, Gypsy stuff, wild and sad. They had parties in their house that lasted for days. It was the best year of his life; it would never get better.

The trade moved from currency to people, groups of refugees laced with fugitives and psychopaths. Now his partners were hard men in slick suits, war criminals missing teeth and limbs. Manuel appeared, stayed with them for three weeks; it occurred to Sestanovich that he was hiding. Helicopters, rejects from the Russian army, passed over his house. At night, while Manuel slept suspended in the rafters of the attic, Sestanovich and his wife swore they heard the mewling of cruel animals stalking the first floor, breaking into the house, crawling up the stairs.

"It was Death," Sestanovich says. "Death coming for us, for the things Manuel had done."

"What had he done?" Wendell says.

No one knew for sure; but a series of murders, stranglings, burnings, dismemberments, were connected to his name. I didn't kill them, Manuel said, I'm not responsible, but you could tell in his head he knew he was. On a night that his wife had gone to visit family, he confronted Manuel in the rafters of his house. What have you gotten us into? Why are you ruining me? But Manuel just shook his head, waved his hands to bat away the questions.

"I will ask you to do one more thing for me," he said. "One more thing, and then I will leave you alone forever."

The crate arrived at the docks of Burgas at two thirty in the morning, conducted to the ship by an operator who ran from the site as soon as his work was done. The crew was Algerian, half of them mercenaries, half of them a radical branch of Sufism that believed in something they called the Descent of the Sky; they would not elaborate. The ship embarked without papers or lights, slipped through the dark water with a silence Sestanovich did not think possible. They were bound for Miami, the captain said. He had no maps, no navigational equipment; he steered by dead reckoning, eyes closed, head tilted back, hands brushing the wheel.

The problems began before they were out of the Mediterranean: two mercenaries, friends for years, hacked each other to pieces with the fire axes in the galley. One of the Sufis hanged himself in the hold. They committed the bodies to the water, assuaged by prayers to Allah.

"We should have turned around then," Sestanovich says. "We should have seen the deaths as signs, as warnings."

But they did not. The Atlantic ate the land behind them, and now they tossed on gray water, a sky that lost its birds, maintained only the strained trails of airplanes too high to see. Three nights from Spain and North Africa, something carried off two Sufis; they found their spines on the deck near the bow, bones threaded with strings of flesh. A leak sprang in the hold. They put a boat down in the water to investigate, a Sufi and a mercenary whose shouts from the ocean's surface could be heard from the captain's post. They returned to the deck; there were gashes in the side of the hull, they said, from the waterline to twenty feet in the air, like a gigantic creature was trying to—

"—Sink the boat?" Sestanovich said.

"No," said the Sufi. "Trying to get in."

The crate, the mercenaries said. It's going to kill us all. That night they fought in the hold, they went at each other with hammers and crowbars while some huge beast pounded at the hull from the outside in the squall of a storm. Three more dead slid into the waves the next day; the prayers for them were suffused with supplication. Allah have mercy. Somebody save us.

"By the end, only I and one of the Algerians remained, mercenary or Sufi or both, I could not guess. The things he had to do, they made him into something else—"

He does not want to talk about it, the death on that ship, of the captain; the weeks at sea clinging to wreckage after the vessel went down with the crate, a heap of bodies, and the ravages of a monster on board. What they say happened to his wife. There is nothing he wants to say about it.

"I came here looking for him," Sestanovich says, "to tell him what happened to his cargo, and to kill him for what he has done to me. But they say now that he is gone and the . . . Horsemen? The Horsemen are killing anyone who knew him . . . they are connected, that crate and these flying men. Death has followed me here. . . ."

And Wendell has a sudden thought, the influence of Lucas Henderson: Death follows us everywhere, he thinks, one step behind us; it is just that some people realize this and some do not.

"Everyone who ever knew Manuel—"

"—But for what?" Wendell says. "What is it that you think he did?"

"Who can know for sure? You have no idea, Captain, the kinds of things he was involved in."

Oh, I have some idea by now, Wendell thinks. He even knew a little before. There were the ornate burns across Manuel's shoulders and back, scarring into indecipherable patterns. He'd watched them rise and fall with sleep under the ambient light of the city while a couple screamed at each other in the next apartment building over.

"What do they mean?" Wendell asked once.

"Nothing."

"Don't lie to me."

"Sometimes," Manuel said, "sometimes I lie to you and sometimes I don't."

"What do the symbols say?"

"I don't know. The artist never got to finish, so it doesn't mean anything yet."

"You're lying again."

"No. Well. Maybe."

But there were other days, Wendell thinks, when Manuel woke up and Wendell was the only one in the world to him. Women gave him the eye and men whistled at his ass, but he'd look only at the man on his arm, leaping onto subways, standing in the sun. He can remember every minute of those days, he knows they ate deviled eggs and woke up somehow in East New York, he remembers how the beams of the Queensboro felt when they jumped from the bridge to the roofs of buses passing below, how the buildings of Midtown shifted past each other as they rode in, how the manholes groaned on the exit ramps, the yellow arrows of constant construction flashed. Storefronts they passed. A shock therapist. A school of theosophy. A Methodist church. His brain clutches at these facts without mercy; but still they're receding from him, moving into shadow.

It hits him then, at last, the cruelty of this. His memory is always pounding his life into a shape, a pattern that points to a conclusion, satisfaction. The final playing out of a theme. The death of his father, the dissolution of his mother, the aimless trips up and down the Eastern seaboard; it is the duty of his brain to resolve all of this into something he can recognize. And for a time, it did: he understood his past as a meandering path, out from the center of suburbia to the people who are not counted, the people on the periphery, until he met a man who did not exist at all. The ideal. The edge of the circle, the end of the line, where Wendell would stop for the first time in twenty-eight years. His memory hacked his past into a thick red line that happened to intersect with Manuel's at just the right time. Had he stayed in the South; had he not gone to New York, waited long enough to allow himself to fall in love with it; had he not met Robert Lord Townsend, Jr., while in line for the sole bathroom at the Maritime Lounge, he never would have heard of Manuel Rodrigo de Guzmán González. The lesson of his history was the joy of having been luck's child, blessed by coincidence. And there was balance: the loss of his family, the gain of this man. Moving, resting. Restlessness; peace.

But his baby's disappearance destroyed this, detonated his head. His memory of security is a mockery to him now. He has been betrayed, he has been fooled, his life demolished without leaving enough behind to build it into consolation. And he still doesn't know why.

Death comes for all of us, he thinks; but I am too angry for it to come for me now.

"They are going after all of us, I think," Sestanovich says. "All of us who knew him. I think maybe they will come for you too, when they learn what you are doing."

"Let them come."

"Can you protect me?"

"That depends."

"On what?"

"Your willingness to be bait."

". . ."

"If they're here for you, they'll find you whether you're hiding or not."

". . ."

"It's stupid to run," Wendell says. You'll live your life in a box, he thinks, always in rooms without windows, your back to the wall, frantic eyes unblinking at the door. Dropping to the floor and whimpering every time a plane flies over you, or the steam heat comes on. A man can't do that for long without dying, he thinks; but ah, here he has already been at it for months.

 Round One

"I feel like chum," Sestanovich says.

There are reports of more killings in Under Brooklyn Heights, in the exits to topside, three men and two women incinerated as they scrambled toward the surface. They say the Horsemen roost in the ceiling of the cavern under Inwood, hanging upside down from their floating craft, raincoats tied around them. Wendell and Masoud have seen them gliding through the gloom in silence, then wheeling starboard and speeding away in spinning formation; but the Horsemen do not come for Sestanovich, and they do not come for Captain Spaceman.

They bring Sestanovich out. They troll Darktown on trawlers and cruisers until everyone knows, everyone is talking about it. They have intense parties at Hyrvygeena, raucous strangers take rounds of vodka with the marked man while teenagers do smack on the metal roof. They rage for hours, until Hackerin' Pete chases them out with an AK-47 because he has to go to sleep sometime. The boys yell at the door, spitting teeth at the Horsemen: come and get us. But they do not come.

"Can you really protect me from them?" Sestanovich says.

"Yes. Yes."

"What if you cannot?"

"We can." But Masoud looks away; he was in firefights before, knows how bad they can go. His brother, twitching in the street, glaring at him from the place in his head. Brother, he thinks, after so many years, does it have to be so hard?

They take Sestanovich, at last, to Darktown Market, during the Festival of Diamond Joe, First Mayor of Darktown: it was he who figured out how to siphon electricity off the city's power grid undetected, he who began suspending everything from the ceiling, worked out the deal with the Koreans to ship the steel cable to do it. The denizens of Darktown re-create his likeness in copper wire festooned with lightbulbs powered by a bicycle generator, it is the head of a parade of New Orleans oompah and Arabic frenzy. Other music follows, rockabilly bands with the guitarist's amp strapped to his back, polkas and reels, a hip-hop group thirty strong, they carry the DJ and his turntables on a platform over their heads and pass the mike around from person to person, so they all get a chance to speak their minds in rhyme. The crowd moves in waves of people, shouting out to their favorites in a wash of corn dogs, sausages, and kimchee. They swarm, a thousand centipedes, through the market, they carry children and the elderly aloft and drop them into the brackish water.

They almost lose Sestanovich to the throng four times, to pulling kids, to the side of a Styrofoam float, twice to sparkplug vendors. Masoud ties Sestanovich to his ankle by a long leather strap he steals from a jouncing cart laden with near-naked people singing and yelling at each other.

"Stay here," he says.

Sestanovich angles nervous glances toward the cavern ceiling.

Nobody is sure who starts it, but somewhere in the upper reaches of the market, in the high scaffolding above Dr. Ease's neon sign, people begin to kiss. They hang along the catwalks, smooching and touching, and now it begins to spread downward, they're pairing off, hands look for hands, eyes meet across the dirty air. Love ripples through the parade, but forms a wake around Wendell, Masoud, and Sestanovich, as if they are on a raft, all alone. Sestanovich thinks of his poor wife back in Slovenia, looking at the river below, the empty dock for the boat they never bought; she must have thought the worst had happened before it did. Masoud is leaving Lebanon yet again, the boys on the deck leaning against machine guns and crying as the ship pulls away. And Wendell, of course he thinks of his baby. They were stumbling back from a night at the Maritime Lounge in the growing light of an early summer dawn, and as they reeled through Carroll Gardens, the sky burst into pink and orange and set the trees on fire, the light poured onto the tops of buildings and fell into the street, and then Manuel pushed him up against the glass of a Laundromat and kissed him, long, so that when it ended, Wendell could think only of wanting more, he was a child again, hungry and needing, and Manuel provided.

The people in love around him grow distant, the walls of

the market stalls buckle and arch away. They are floating twelve feet above all this, they see it through thick smog, and Wendell softens the impulse to just keep rising, out of the cavern, through the concrete and steam pipes and into the night. All must seem peaceful from high above, the lights and commotion reduced to a steady burn, the glow of a fire far away.

Honey. Honey baby. Where are you?

There is the screech of aircraft, a yowl from above. The couples break apart, children scatter, the music crashes into disorder as the Four Horsemen sway overhead and descend on the crowd, pulling their weapons from their raincoats. Sestanovich yelps and takes off, vaulting over the rushing throng. His leash plays out singing, tightens, cracks to its full length. Sestanovich jerks back, Masoud jerks forward, but Sestanovich's adrenaline has the better of him now, the better of them both, and Masoud is dragged along the floor as Sestanovich takes to the scaffolding, clambers arm over arm into the steel beams until Masoud is his anchor and he can go no farther; he hangs there, screaming, but nobody can hear him because Wendell has produced two submachine guns, has them leveled at the Horsemen and is spitting bullets. They trace through the smoke and stutter into the giants, bounce shrieking off the hulls of their craft, but the Horsemen pass unperturbed; they head straight for Sestanovich, weapons bared, whining as they warm up.

The grenade gets their attention; it knocks the second Horseman off its craft and sends the rider plummeting into a hardware stand. The craft wheels in circles, looking for its owner as Wendell leaps onto the downed giant, puts a pistol to its head, and fires. But the giant just kicks him off, sends him into a pile of stolen hammers. It gets up, emits a steady tone, and the craft whirs toward it; but as it remounts, Wendell grabs one of its legs and is dragged into the air. Now the other three have wheeled around, they've never had this happen before, and they're taking careful aim, trying to incinerate Wendell off the bottom of the scooter. But Wendell already has his legs wrapped around the engine and is using his free hand to send seventy-six rounds into the third Horseman, who jerks in his seat but remains there, lets go with something that sounds almost like laughter.

Who are these people? Wendell thinks.

A Horseman draws close, grabs Wendell by the waist and pries him off the bottom of the car, then hefts him over its head. Wendell unsheathes a knife strapped to his calf, swings at the arm, and cuts off what looks like a hand, causing Wendell and the body part to fall twenty feet through canvas stalls and wooden beams to land, as luck would have it, in a pillow stand.

The four now swarm toward Sestanovich, whom Masoud has pulled down from the rafters: the two of them run, maniacs, clawing over people to get away. Masoud unleashes a semiautomatic into the head of the lead Horseman, but they just toss him away when they reach him. Their weapons whine to life and fire; Sestanovich screams and soils himself, but the green flames leap over him and settle on someone else, who flares like a firework and vanishes. Two more, in black-and-white robes, dash for the water. One is cremated before she gains eight yards; the other they catch in middive; the robes become fire, then steam as the man hits the water. The four circle the place where he vanished, then spiral upward into the darkness; the sounds of their engines dissipate above, and all is quiet.

The man thrashes to the surface, his robes dark with blood and burn; he gives off the smell of cooking. Masoud and Wendell are the first ones there, they pull him onto the platform, where he sputters, breathes out blood.

"I saw you fighting them . . . ," he says. ". . . Did the High Epopt send you to protect us? . . ."

"High Epopt, what's the—?"

"—Of the Church of Panic, the High . . ."

Wendell and Masoud look at each other.

"They've come to get us all, all of us . . ." He settles into incoherence, a blind stare, his tongue moving against his teeth without forming words. But his hands move within his robes, produce the silver scroll containing charts they do not understand, but a list that they do.

"All of us . . ."

They had no idea the Church of Panic had so many members: it looks like over a thousand, split up into trios. Names, addresses. From East New York to the Upper East Side, speaking a hundred and two languages. A catholic faith. But here, here, on every page, seven or eight of them have been crossed out: deaths, dozens of them already, near the sewage treatment plant in Greenpoint, in the Hasidic neighborhood in Bay Ridge, deaths in the South Bronx and Brighton Beach. A massacre in Darktown. If the newspapers knew, it'd be on the front page. But nobody like that knows, not reporters or police or the doctors in emergency rooms. The damage is too complete: green fire, and there is not enough ash to dirty a sidewalk. The people are too unknown. You don't die, you disappear. All these people. The Church of Panic has been on the run for days, in storage bins, in Dumpsters; they lose themselves in a city underground. But the Horsemen are finding them all the same, and the list gets smaller and smaller.

Masoud is skimming through the pages, gives a sudden frown. "Wendell," he says. "Lucas's name is on here."

Manuel's is not.

 ## We Are Not Angry at You

Diane has not seen Lucas in fifteen days. She thought she saw him in Midtown, clad in robes and floating down the sidewalk, but could not be sure; she is seeing less and less of the Church of Panic these days. Erwin Gruenwald stopped writing epic poetry about cellular phones, switched to shorter and shorter works that have grown more paranoid. He was down to four-syllable rants for a while that had the eerie, alien quality of brilliant insanity, but is now reduced to one-syllable words printed on calling cards. Hide. Leave. Flee.

In her dreams, she and Lucas embrace in a nighttime landscape of wind-thrashed corn eleven feet high while giant shapes move above them. His lips taste of citrus and bitter alcohol, and he does not resist when her arms make clear that she will not let him go. It seems like they kiss for days, but she always wakes up before dawn, with the Ecuadorians around her in a ring, turning in fits. Last week a man calling himself the Space Cowboy sprinted onto the runway at JFK to catch a ride to the stratosphere, as he put it. He succeeded in lassoing a plane's landing gear as it folded into the body; then the craft's gathering speed dragged him into the exhaust chamber, where the predictable occurred. The Ecuadorians have begun calling in sick to look for other work, but the talk among the immigrants on the curb, waiting for the contractors in their red pickups and blue vans, bothers them. Men are going back early, they say. There are rumors of disease here, an epidemic that will clog the city with corpses. A war is coming. We are going back, some of the day laborers say. The finca is terrible, we are treated like slaves, but there are fewer fanatics. Only idiots go back to the fincas, the others say. They'll take their chances on the pestilence. The Ecuadorians return to the airport, try not to shake hands with new workers so much, avoid the busy terminals where passengers from all over the world are breathing, leaving traces of spittle on airport glasses. They won't go anywhere near the bathrooms.

"Maybe we should have left sooner," one of them says.

"Yes," another says. "Just like our Lavinia."

Lavinia, the wife of El Flaco, whom they knew as the queen of the soccer festivals, the one who bent down, draped their shoulders with ribbons and medals, anointed them each with a kiss on the forehead before declaring them the best players in the city, better than the Dominicans, better even than the Brazilians, who always claimed the title was theirs. They knew her also from the bar made of corrugated metal cut out of the side of an auto body repair shop in the Iron Triangle, a place of painted signs and unpaved ground in the shadow of Shea Stadium that reminded the Ecuadorians of the places they were from. The bottles of beer steamed with cold as they came out of the refrigerator, warmed in the hand, and the Ecuadorians cooled their throats as Lavinia began to speak. At first it was about rent, neighborhood feuds, who hated whom, small stories from the smuggling trade that did not risk sentencing people to death. But she was always a lightweight, and two beers later her stories spiraled toward home. This was the raw truth: this city afflicted her with a deep unhappiness. In the winter this place is a meat locker, she said. In the spring it is an open sewer, and by the end of the summer it is a crematorium. That's why everyone who can leave gets out, and some new batch of suckers moves in, because they don't know, they are unprepared.

She took, at last, another sip of warm beer. "We've been here a long time, we let the city take our youth from us. We're not cowards if we give up now." And began to cry.

But the Ecuadorians do not want to give up. They like this city. Back home, they had already saved places for them on the fincas, they took away their desks in school because they thought the four of them were bound only for work, forty years in fields and processing plants, swinging in a harness from a crane, throwing fruit on a truck, and then an early death, worn out and stretched thin, covered in newspapers reporting the murders of union organizers. There was a place in front of the church marked for their bodies to fall alongside their fathers, spitting blood from a dozen holes; then a hollow under a mahogany in the rain forest for them to release a last malarial breath. Then death in the mines, death on the road, asphyxiation in Virginia. But look, look, they escaped all of that. They are here at the airport, they save their paychecks, one day they will move into plumbing or car repair, they will wear slacks and button-down shirts and have an office behind a pane of glass. They will buy two-story houses and new cars at cost, and when they retire, they will travel across the United States; they will return to Guatemala, to Ecuador, and buy land, a small fruit plantation, farm equipment, two delivery trucks, they will hire more men to work alongside them and prosper. And when they retire to a hammock on the coast, they will send mocking pictures to immigration authorities, the Guatemalan army, and the Ecuadorian government, financial statements with nasty drawings in the margins. You sold us out early, but we were better than that. See how you cut us short; see how we rose above.

In the morning, they sense Diane's distance. She is good to them, but they have lost her: she wants a pair of arms that does not belong to any of them.

"Diane," one of them says, "You have been generous with us, but your heart is not here now. Is it."

"No," she says, "it's not."

"Then go," another says. "We are angry at the rest of the world, but never at you."

She moves to each of them, puts a kiss on each forehead, brings them close for as long as they need, as long as she needs.

"I love you all," she says.

"We love you too," they say.

A Night to Be Happy

Lucas's apartment has been deserted. The onions are rotting, the milk is going bad. Dust gathers on the tops of books, the seat of the couch, the covers of the bed. Over a week's worth of mail is jammed into the mailbox, a small pile of envelopes is growing on the floor, bank offers, a coupon book, a jury-duty notice. Cockroaches and mice are recolonizing the gouged floor, in a day there will be war between the species that the cockroaches will win through sheer numbers, beginning by infesting the easy chair facing the window. When the fighting has ended, the living room will be spotted with the corpses of combatants, but nobody will bury them; the superintendent is a lax man who almost never ventures up to Lucas's floor, and Lucas himself will not return. No. He and four Church of Panic members are hiding in a bunker with canned goods, under a false floor in a South Bronx warehouse. For seventy-five dollars they got the owner to park his semi over the hatch. But it will not be enough.

There used to be nine of them, fleeing north in a 2 train, but the Horsemen caught up at 135th Street, peeled off the roof of the car and leapt inside as the train barreled on, and the train stopped shy of Jackson Avenue. Passengers panicked and cried, ducked, curled up into the seats shielding their children as the lights in the car flickered out, but the Horsemen didn't mind, they could see their targets clear enough. They incinerated the first two in seconds as the others scrambled through the doors between cars; they got another one as Lucas pried open the doors to the tracks outside. The Horsemen pegged two more as they fled up the stairs of the Jackson Avenue station, and there the police managed to slow the assassins down, the giants roaring at the cops with a metallic scream and pinwheeling down the tracks, leaving the privates, just boys from Katonah Avenue who flirted with the Irish girls on the weekends, scratching their scalps. Testimony was extracted from the terrified witnesses in the subway car, who told some incoherent story about raincoats and someone being burned to a cinder, though there was no evidence of this. In the end, it's a quarter of a column in the *Daily News,* it's on the books as a police investigation, it backs up subway traffic for angry commuters, who assume it's a drunk yowling on the platform or someone pushed on the tracks.

Wendell and Masoud have been keeping vigil on Lucas's rooftop for four days. They have slept in shifts; they've climbed down the fire escape to peer into the windows, to make sure that Lucas did not come and go. Inspector Trout has come twice. The first time he rang the buzzer, then stood on the stoop examining his fingernails for nine minutes before leaving. The second time he came with papers, made the superintendent ascend to Lucas's apartment for the first time in years. Trout strolled around the apartment, eyeing the rodent bodies. He made a phone call and left. Last night, Diane came by, took shy steps to the door, rang and waited, rang and waited. She gazed from window to window, believing she saw light or movement; she called up to the apartment, cupping her hands to let the yearning stay in her voice as she said his name, so that if he were sleeping, she might pull him out, bring him down the stairs to her. At last, she leapt to the metal ladder on the side of the building and climbed the fire escape. She knocked on the window and stayed there crouching for a long time; and Wendell watched her from less than fifteen feet above, the shifting of her legs, the movement of her head, trying to peer into the dark. He recognized the stubbornness in her, the refusal to give in. He wanted to whisper to her, make her look up, tell her that he understood, but of course he could not; he was supposed to be dead.

It is now Friday night—no, it must be Saturday morning, for over on Conover Street, the first crowd of partiers spills out of the Maritime Lounge, their shouts and hollers mixing with the raw old-time country music and the shots of an old car backfiring, a stereo springing to life and hunkering out Romanian dance music, percussion slithering and pounding under manic horns. Someone gets off a single firework that slides into the sky and explodes over the neighborhood, snowing sparks of green and yellow, and everyone cheers. Both Wendell and Masoud remember nights like that, running down the cobbled street laughing and mad, brain and muscles on fire, plugged into the crackling wire of this place, crazy with the faith that at any second, anything could happen, anything at all; but that seems distant to them now. They are watching from above, as aliens might, the movement of humans through the streets, and they are benevolent and generous, but they do not understand it, not anymore. Across the river, the buildings are dark and far away; the party in the street is dispersing, the partiers are thinning out to look for more drugs, to sleep with someone, and the noise settles down into the thrumming hush that is always in the background here, a low whisper that keeps out-of-towners awake for hours but works like a lullaby on the people who live here.

Wendell gives a sudden laugh. *"Play* it? As soon as I get these pajamas off, I'm gonna *fuck* it."

Masoud laughs.

"See, you didn't have to start over."

". . ."

". . ."

"The Horsemen are not coming," Masoud says. "Or they came already and left."

"They might still come."

"Maybe."

"What do you think it means that Manuel's name is not on the list?" Masoud says.

"I don't know."

Masoud open his mouth to speak again, but thinks better of it. The words to follow would be unkind. Maybe it means they got him already, that he was in that apartment after all, when the Horsemen visited it. Maybe it means there is no connection at all, that Wendell has done all of this for nothing, chasing a fiction.

"Are you sorry you did this?" Masoud says.

"No."

"You have given up so much to find him. What will you say to him when you see him again?"

"I don't know. I haven't really thought about it."

"You are risking death at the hands of four demons to find him, and you haven't—"

"—I'm not going to say anything. I just want to know why he left."

"And if he left for someone else?"

"He didn't."

"He had other—"

"—I know. But he didn't leave for someone else."

"How do you know?"

"Why are you asking me this now? Are you leaving me now too?"

Again Masoud wants to speak. He wants to tell Wendell that he will never leave. That he is in awe of his devotion. That Wendell is perhaps the most remarkable man Masoud has ever met. But it is too much to speak of these things, it goes too far.

"No," Masoud says. "I am not leaving."

". . ."

". . ."

"Do you think they'll come?" Wendell says.

"I do not know."

"Do you think we'll find him?"

Masoud does not answer, but his arm reaches out, his hand falls on Wendell's shoulder and stays there. Lights are moving along the edge of Manhattan, lights are moving in the harbor; down below, a new crowd is streaming toward the Maritime Lounge, they're already piss-drunk and ecstatic, they spin in the street and laugh to wake the neighborhood. This is happening everywhere tonight, it is a night to be happy, there are people animated by chemicals and company that drive off sleep, they are ready to dance for six more hours. Somewhere there are bands who are just getting warmed up, bands who haven't started playing yet, who will be heard only by those lucky enough to be there, limbs ready to move, throat ready to unleash howls when each number is done. They are living hours tonight that they will return to fifty-seven years from now, when Death is coming for them. They will remember how the band played and how they moved, or the way that girl moved, they will hang their pride on the faith that it was good enough; that they lived enough, that they were here. But they do not think of that now. They have no idea what's coming.

CHAPTER 6

In Which Decisions Are Made, and There Is Violence

 Wendell's Dream #3

Fifty-one. Fifty. Forty-nine.

Stop.

Uno, dos, tres, cuatro—

He begins inside the bass drum, the giant mallet swinging toward his head and away, toward and away, muffled by an old shirt. But already he is floating out and up; there's the band, ah, do you know what you can do with your funk, Star Child? and the crowd has its hands in the air. Singers, horns, all moving in front of microphones. It's a party, y'all, and we're all invited. But he has already drifted up through the ceiling, there is the uncomfortable feeling of passing through asbestos, and on the floor above, two teenagers are going at it on the rug, in time to the music—the boy doesn't have more than two minutes left in him, he's only seventeen, for God's sake—the next floor is wooden crates, the next filled with beanbags, nobody knows why; and then he passes through the roof with a shiver and rises between buildings, gaining speed, he's a quarter of a mile up, now half, and now the outlines of the islands appear in burning phosphorus, Long Island arches in like a fish, coming to the mainland to eat.

The sun draws a crescent of fire along the edge of the planet. Dead communication satellites swing by, run through by pellets of meteorites. Birds and airplanes are far below. He is by himself in this place, where the air thins, grows cold. There is ice on his clothes, ice in his lungs; his breath shudders to a stop.

Forty-eight. Forty-seven.

Dearest love, my only boy. Why did you go?

Oye, Hombre

When the grandchildren that survive ask him about it years later—when did you know?—Salmon will recall this day, the day the phone rang and rang with report after report and was still ringing long after they left, messages toppling onto each other, never seen anything like them, what are they, must come help now, while Salmon and Trout tore from neighborhood to neighborhood, never turning off the siren, saw more death in one day than they ever had before, than they ever thought they would again. If only those terrified people had come to us, he will think, there would have been something we could have done to protect them.

It starts at three in the morning, frantic phone calls about flying machines, five people burned to death in the street, balls of green flame scorching the sides of buildings, charred plants on the windowsill. Seven minutes later, three people are cremated behind a Dumpster in Cypress Hills. Nine minutes after that, eight people are cut in half on 141st Street in front of a Baptist church, several onlookers watch the craft sweep into the sky, spiraling in formation. At last, the public spectacle that brings television reporters to the scene, to Trout and Salmon's empty office. On Broadway, heading toward Union Square, eleven people are chased down one by one by the four marauders, each turned to ash by a lancing arc of energy, near misses peeling off the roofs of cars, melting manhole covers, maiming the unlucky. It lasts for only minutes, but the reports go on for hours, crying people, hysterical, three men on the corner pointing at the place above the street where the craft flew, did you fucking see it? Amateur photos, two video cameras, the reporters already in the realm of hyperbole, spending ammunition that will leave them mute later. Outside Trout and Salmon's office, the clot of newsmen gets bigger, they want to talk to the cops who, the police chief says, have been following this, the ones who understand best what is happening. But they cannot find them. Trout and Salmon are in Jackson Heights; no, they're on Ocean Parkway; no, they're in Bed-Stuy.

No. They're standing in the intersection of 108th and Amsterdam, two police vans around them, a small contingent of uniforms, and they are both crouching down, trying to keep everyone quiet, for they have at last found a man who survived. His legs, the lower part of his torso, are blackened and reek of meat; his arms lay bent at odd angles, he oozes blood into the gutter. His tongue moves without sound, but his eyes stare at the two investigators with urgency.

"You're from the Church of Panic, aren't you," Salmon says.

The head nods; the throat coughs.

"You know why this is happening." Trout says.

Again, the nod. A cough, and then one word: "Lavinia . . ."

There will be thirty-eight more crime scenes today, more charred corpses and heaps of ash, but it is this one that Salmon will remember. The man's voice gives out after that, he cannot speak, has trouble breathing, they load him into the ambulance and take him to St. Luke's, where he will die two hours later after desperate operations to save him.

Salmon turns around once, sweating through his suit, to regard the intersection. The neighborhood has gathered to see what is coming for them, they stand sweltering on the sidewalk in thin pants, wide-collared shirts. People lean out of windows. He hears whispers in Spanish, whispers in four different

African languages, and behind them, there is music: Cuba wafts from the barbershop where they've stopped cutting hair, men with half-shaved heads stand in the doorway; there is Ethiopian music from an apartment somewhere, and under them, the chatter of percussion from a deli, from cars, from places he will never see. Then, there is a shout from the rooftop by a fifteen-year-old in a drenched T-shirt—

"—*Oye! Oye, hombre!* Get 'em, *hombre!* Get 'em!"

The heads all nod, there are almost smiles, as if all of them wanted to say that. And Salmon feels honored, he knows what some of these people have seen, what they came from, he knows so many of the things that happen to them here, he reads reports that make his stomach curl, but here they all are, smoking and cutting hair, saving money in cardboard boxes, going to parties that remind them of the place they came from. People are so resilient, he thinks. They will survive this. They can survive anything.

 Big Love

The Pan-Galactic Groove Squad, with equipment, takes up a third of a subway car. The other two-thirds fills up with people who become fans. They feel the love off this band even when they're not playing; it's just a love in repose, a softer thing.

The Squad began at a party, it was just one woman riffing

on an acoustic guitar. What it was she was playing none of them can remember now, but soon a man beating his hands on the table joined her, while another started pounding the floor. Then came the singers, someone who made a quick bass from a broomstick, cord, and a washbucket he found in the kitchen. Soon there were twenty of them or so, all smiling at each other. They were all on the same planet from hour one. Other guests came, danced, and left, came and danced, and left sweating and flush with the funk, but the musicians remained; soon it was only the twenty-three of them and they showed no sign of stopping, though the host went out to a bar to drink and locked them out of the bathroom. At last, sometime around noon the next day, someone got too hungry and stopped, and at that they all dropped out, one by one, until it was back to the guitar again, only now she was playing something that nobody but the other twenty-two could read. She put her pick down, rubbed her raw fingers in her palm, and said, people, we should be a band.

They live as a collective in a warehouse they call the Hive on the end of Greenpoint by the sewage treatment facility; their neighbors throw barbecues on their rickety roof and are up there until five in the morning, playing the Minutemen amid the luscious smell of caramelized onions while they toss beer bottles and watermelon rinds into the truck depot below. The warehouse is one giant room and until a few months ago was a flurry of chaos and groove, cooking and playing, cleaning and playing, fixing the ceiling and playing; none of them ever slept more than three hours a night.

But life at the Hive has changed. They play less, they sleep even less; they spend more time staring out the windows, watching the skyscrapers across the river and the tops of the buildings around them. They are responding to the vibe in the city these days; under the frenzy, the mad rush, the drive and change, there is nervousness. Anxiety. And now the incinerations in the street, the four craft that the news still can't identify: the rumors say the Army is testing new equipment, or no, the CIA. It's terrorism again. It's organized crime. Nobody really knows. Explosions rise from the city, balls of green flame. The military helicopters brought in to bring down the Four Horsemen meander over the boroughs, lost and confused.

"Maybe," one of the bass players says, "we should seek our groove on another longitude."

A trumpet player thinks. "Yes. Roam the earth like our heroes do."

"Praise Bootsy." The bass player bows his head.

"San Francisco, Atlanta, Seattle."

"The Florida Panhandle. New Orleans."

"Vladivostok. Bangkok. Calcutta. Samarkand."

"Spreading the gospel of funk."

"We could."

A drummer interjects. "Brothers, I am down with the things you say. Let me make but one reply." He takes them up to the patched roof and turns them around, three hundred sixty degrees, through Brooklyn, Manhattan, the Bronx, Queens, even Staten Island, and back again. A gout of flame rises, forty blocks away, the helicopters swarm around it, but then stop; already, the Horsemen have gone.

"All these people you would give up for lost, when they need the groove the most."

For a time, the bass and trumpet players are silent, regarding the islands, the heat rising off the buildings, the smoke dissipating in the air, the dark water. All those people.

"We will stay," says the bass player, and the trumpet player agrees. They will stay.

Six years later, they will be flung across the globe; they will pass under thick vines on a splintered raft on the Orinoco; wrap themselves in tan linen and lurch across the Maghreb on a camel with five others who do not speak their language. They will sleep in Buddhist monasteries hidden in the mountains that slide into Lake Biwa, build houses in the branches of sequoias, dig burrows in the earth of the Ferghana Valley, carry their homes on tarps rolled on their backs until they've followed the blasted highways across the Atacama, slide down the great dunes to nest in the ruins of Antofagasta. None of them will ever see any of the others again, and that loss will rupture stomachs, shove a shunt into skulls. But they will not regret that they stayed so long, that they were among the last across the river, the last into the trains, into the antique propeller planes. They will always hear it in the creaking sway of trees, in the pulse of surf, the cough of engines turning over, their own footsteps in the dirt, in the lean music the people around them make at night when they can't go another hour without partying, in all of it they will always hear the rushing blood of their brothers and sisters, the Squad's deep groove, and from it each of them will be able to pull out all the others, to gather the band around them, count off the measure for nothing, and build the city again, wherever they go.

Forty-six. Forty-five.

 That Ugly Specimen

Eight hundred sixty-five miles away, the corpse that tangled in the pier in the Financial District lies, plaid shirt removed, on a white table under the lamps of a plastic-clad pathologist at the Centers for Disease Control. He prods a piece of the body with a speculum, incises with a scalpel. They run tests, take fluid samples and put them through a centrifuge. They examine tissue samples through an electron microscope, do everything they can to convince themselves that there is evidence to support some documentable truth.

Dr. Gore, you see, refused to voice the wild thought in her head, had the body sent to another hospital. Let them lose their minds with it, she thought, let me retain my sanity, my faith in my training. From hospital to hospital the body was shuffled, the documentation attached to the cadaver lengthening, the incredulity in the reports palpable even in the detached manner of autopsy. Maintenance of composition noted despite lack of attempts at preservation. Abnormal physiology; superlative adverbs accrued to the front of this phrase. Necessity of tracing cadaver to source. Must send samples to more sophisticated research site. Library of tissue necessary to determine. At last, the cadaver was pushed into the back of an ambulance—peculiar odor noted—and brought to Army Medical Research in Washington. There, a rising young pathologist known at the facility for his candor summed up the mood in frank utterances, written in his histrionic hand: What is this? Where did it come from?

The CDC's pathologist, as the last to examine it before pronouncing the mad verdict, was allowed to wax rapturous. Seven careers' worth of research on the spleen alone, if spleen it is, she wrote. Heart, if heart it is, like nothing I've ever seen. Would take half the years off my life to see a live specimen. She had no doubt that it spoke, moved, was capable of complex thought. I know where it's *not* from.

But the wake of papers that makes its way to Dr. Gore's mailbox is long in coming, as doctor after doctor needs to make sure, rules out every alternative and is still not satisfied; is unwilling to call on the telephone, the solution too strange to speak it aloud. The practice of medicine is unprepared, its practitioners are not ready, though they will have to be soon, when It happens and they are working in basements and boiler rooms, or in mobile hospital units installed on the insides of old armored cars. Then they will have to learn. The first letter, from the Army pathologist, will reach Dr. Gore's hands in a day, but by then there will be little for her to do but call the police, sweep all the medical supplies she can into a garbage bag, and run for home.

Our Hero, Part 3

Inspector Trout does not understand them yet, does not see how they work, but he has made the connections on a piece of paper that he carries in his pocket. Already it is a spider-web: strands connecting Manuel, Wendell, Masoud, and Lucas, each one to the other; then a line from Lucas to the Church of Panic, the Church to the Four Horsemen, and the Four Horsemen back to Wendell, for, yes, the news had reached the surface that it was they who had done Wendell in, his ashes lying in a sad corner somewhere, tracked by roaches under heavy machinery. A dotted line runs from the Horse-men to Manuel, a small question mark over it; and hovering over the diagram, the name Lavinia, squiggling lines to Manuel, to the Church, to the Horsemen, and above it, a big question mark: Why?

He has come back to Lucas's apartment to find out. Lucas Henderson has not appeared in the street, scorched or turned to ash; he has not arrived at the morgue. Trout is betting that he's still alive. He remembers the way Lucas spoke in the interviews following Manuel's disappearance: serious, words of burning clarity. A strength there, a fire, this was a resourceful man, someone who knew how to protect him-self. So Trout waits, he stations himself on the stoop across the street, elbows resting on knees. Cars, buses, trundle by, men and women with bags, talking in low voices, people are leaning on windowsills, blaring radios, it's a normal summer day on this block in Red Hook; but then a helicopter roams overhead, guns loaded, or there is the dull shudder of another explosion, a reminder. He thinks of his partner, chasing fireballs. Salmon will hear about another victim left alive to answer their questions; and then the squad car will race down Columbia to find him, Salmon will be out of the vehicle before it stops, his head on fire, for all has been revealed to him. It will be so much stranger than what is on the piece of paper in Trout's pocket, the diagram there is just the little toe, and as Salmon traces the giant body in the air, Trout will feel the old beat returning, he will interject, introduce ideas into the stream. Soon they will be riffing again, stringing phrases one after the other until nobody can understand what they're saying anymore, it'll be just the two of them, tracking the shape of the biggest plot they've ever seen; and he will have his friend again.

An hour passes. There are more explosions, four in quick succession, as if the Horsemen are demolishing an entire block. Machine guns answer back—ah, they've brought in special units at last, Trout thinks. Or the National Guard. Or maybe the Horsemen attacked the wrong block, it's a neighborhood where the populace happen to bear heavy arms. He imagines the awkwardness of having to arrest those men if they brought the Horsemen down. Thank you for saving our city from assault; please come with us and hand over your weapons to be destroyed. How embarrassing for the police to be so many steps behind. But that happens all the time, he thinks. Life races ahead of us, and we clutch at the scraps that remain; we figure out the story long after it's over.

It's then that he sees Diane, peering at the sky, her steps goaded by desire, weighted by exhaustion, looking for the one she loves. She begins, again, the routine that is approaching ritual: first she stands in front of the building and stares up at the windows, looking for a sign; then she checks the mail, notices how the pile has grown and now includes a letter from his parents marked *Urgent!* in big red letters on the front and back, decorated with symbols she does not recognize. She tries the buzzer, tries it again; waits. And Trout can see it in her shoulders, the ebbing of hope, the sudden dreadful way that your life can expand before you, all the yearning of childhood and coming illnesses of old age descend into your head, people around you move without purpose. You will never get what you want, and your heart grows tired of trying.

Explosions from the projects a quarter of a mile away send men and women into the street; they watch the plumes of smoke rise and curdle in the summer heat. She goes to mount the fire escape—and at last, at last, he appears, a sooty hand reaching from the debris in the alley, and now all of him: Lucas Henderson, deprogrammed from the Lunar Temple, one of the last surviving members of the Church of Panic, a man who has hidden in the belching chimney of an incinerator, who has wrapped himself in plastic and lain under the surface of the Gowanus Canal for fifteen hours, breathing through a piece of piping while the four craft sped overhead, screaming like metallic vultures, who has seen sixteen people reduced to cinders. The High Epopt himself, who wore red sneakers in second grade and ate the macaroni instead of gluing it, who crawled with him under the compound fence to buy cigarettes off the boys who climbed up the mountain from town to sell them—the High Epopt burst into flame atop a water tower in Fort Greene and fell thrashing into the street below. Lucas wears the remains of his friends in his clothes, his hair and skin are singed with the heat of so many near misses, his legs rattle with fatigue when he is not running, and he pulls Diane off the fire escape now, tells her he's only trying to protect her. At first she protests, raises her voice, but he puts a hand over her mouth, tells her they must be quiet or they'll both die; and she puts her arms around him, brings him in very close, and whispers something in his ear that Trout cannot hear.

"Lucas Henderson," Trout calls out.

Lucas swings around, wild, panicked.

"Mr. Henderson . . ."

"Shut up! Shut up or we'll all—"

"—I have been trying to find you for—"

"—Shut—"

Too late again: there is the sound of incoming aircraft, an unearthly scream, and a bolt of green fire streaks over their heads and bores a hole in the sidewalk. Lucas tries to run, but his legs have had enough; he stumbles, begins to pull himself along with his arms.

"Run . . . ," he says. But Diane will not move.

Trout is ready. At the age of sixteen, he was almost killed in his car, crushed by a pickup from one side and a school bus full of children from the other. The accident promised to be awful, all three vehicles demolished, the wrenched metal, the limbs on the road, the death toll more than a small town in Michigan was made to bear. Had he panicked or lost his concentration, it would have come to pass. But time slowed for him: the motion of the scissoring vehicles was delayed, and his muscles moved deliberate and sure, the way out revealed itself to him in the closing space of air. He executed a turn meant for stunt drivers without sweating, prevented himself from driving into a ditch. His pulse never changed, his breathing held constant. And so it is now. The Four Horsemen are bearing down on him; it is a simple thing to draw his gun and fire, fire again, aim for the places where their flapping raincoats move the least: their heads, their torsos. Another lance of green flame puts a hole at his feet, and he fires four more times at the lead vehicle, which bucks, stalls, then dives straight for the ground, the driver too stunned to stop it; it explodes on impact, a round sphere of expanding blue energy that pops into steam. But before the crowd that's gathering in the street can cheer, the giant strides from the wreckage, unharmed, it seems, and now draws a weapon from its coat, aims it at Trout with the same calm ease that the detective sees in himself. Six more rounds do nothing, and Trout gets a chance to think, ah, so this is how I go.

Thirty-eight. Thirty-seven.

Then, from out of nowhere, six Black & Decker circular saws cut the giant into seven discrete sections. The head and torso trace separate arcs to the sidewalk, while the two arms and three legs spin in the air for a few yards before falling into the street. The head lets out what must be a curse as the torso attempts to squirm toward it, and already the five limbs are getting their bearings, moving toward the trunk, but almost nobody notices that, for already another set of saws has dismembered a Horseman in flight; shedding limbs and head, the craft carries the torso over the rooftops and into the harbor, down to the muddy bottom with the remains of the Native Americans sacrificed to an island paid for in seashells and devalued currency.

The people in the street stare, agog. Others appear in windows, in doorways; all heads turn to the top of Lucas's building, all eyes rest on the one who must have thrown the blades, who has done what the police, National Guard, and organized crime could not.

"Who are you?" someone calls out.

Wendell allows himself a quick smile as he pulls his crossbow from his back, a smile for the ludicrous sense that he's really a hero now, like in stories you tell to children to give them courage against imaginary fears.

"I'm Captain Spaceman," he says.

But his mission is only half done. The two remaining Horsemen speed toward him, engines whining; and Wendell impales one with a crossbow bolt tethered to a steel cable. The Horsemen arc skyward and Wendell is carried aloft, but his training with the Ciphers has prepared him well: he climbs arm over arm up the tether, and, before the giant can respond, cuts off its arms with a machete. His legs now planted on the vehicle, he beheads the giant and tosses the body onto a rooftop below. He turns the craft around to engage his last opponent; but the fourth Horseman is already plummeting earthward, toward the space between the buildings where Lucas is still trying to regain his feet, where Trout is reloading his semiautomatic and Diane stands, paralyzed not by fear, but because she has waited far too long to let Lucas go now.

Masoud appears on the rooftop with something he brought over piece by piece from Lebanon: a Russian-made mortar that hasn't been fired in years, but manages to put a shell into the last Horseman's face all the same. The craft wheels, an attempt to dodge; and it is all the time Wendell needs to catch up and slice the last Horseman in half. Its craft smashes through the roof of the warehouse next to Lucas's building, and the torso, head and arms attached, falls into the street, where it begins dragging itself toward its disassembled comrades, yelling at them in its steel voice, desperate, defeated.

The gathered crowd loses control, they whoop and holler, they kiss strangers in the street. Music erupts from everywhere, and soon everyone is dancing, the apartments empty out, people come running for blocks around until Van Brunt is filled up to the entrance of the Battery Tunnel, people singing and clapping while the military helicopters hover overhead and the police try in vain to get through. The news flies down to Darktown that Captain Spaceman won, and parties light up throughout the caverns and catacombs; money changes hands, the ones who bet on the underdog head to Hyrvygeena and buy Hackerin' Pete out of booze, they emerge from manholes, their clothes stuffed with bills, and buy the first thing they see, cars, streetlamps, apartment buldings, they take beautiful women they've just met to dinners that cost more than they've spent in a month. And the Ciphers, who happen to have gambled almost everything they had on the success of their protégé, return to the suspended tugboat with eighteen suitcases full of cash. They all smile and nod at each other, for they knew their son could do it; they put their new names on perfect forgeries of birth certificates and driver's licenses, take their shares, and prepare to walk proud, arm in arm, to the surface. They will never go back.

Wendell lands next to the last Horseman struggling across the pavement to find its other half. The head squeals at him, a voice to shred eardrums, but Wendell doesn't care. His house has been destroyed. He has been halfway to the bottom of the Hudson, almost turned to cinder underground. He has severed himself from what remained of his bombed-out life and made himself anew. He has come for answers, to comprehend why his baby left him; but, pulling back the piece of cloth covering the head of this crawling torso, he does not understand.

It is not fair. He has done it all for nothing, for a head that is not a head, that is nothing he can recognize, nothing he is prepared to fathom. Not yet.

"Wendell Apogee," Lucas says. "I knew you could not be dead."

Wendell turns to him and Lucas winces, for the hurt is so great in the man before him, so great already.

"I know where Manuel is," he says.

CHAPTER 7

In Which All Is Revealed

 Abracadabra

The earth spins in orbit, whirls clouds in Asia into cyclones, throws winds across the Sahara, whips waves into white froth on the Pacific, practicing for tsunamis. On the dark side of the planet, the lights of coastal cities draw the edge of the continent, a sharp line against black water, first blotted by thunderheads, then by satellites, the Moon; then by something else, indistinct, silent. On the side lit by sun, it is more obvious. There is still no sound, but projected shadows writhe on the planet's surface, creating small eclipses that betray the objects moving closer, shapes in space that people in the Great

Plains, driving on the highways headed east, lying on the roofs of buildings in Jersey, crossing streets on wide avenues might see, if they would only look up.

Thirty. Twenty-nine.

Dr. Gore's hand sweats against the receiver, a signal flashes down the wire, twisting through the wall, lancing under the sidewalk, darting into the precinct building, to explode into Salmon's phone. It rings, rattles, for the hundred and seventeenth time, she leaves another frantic message, pick up if you're there, oh God you've got to pick up—

Twenty-eight. Twenty-seven.

The party in Red Hook is getting out of control, it spreads away from Van Brunt to the old piers in the gasoline-laced water, to the municipal swimming pool and the soccer fields, it reaches into the projects and pulls men and women out of their apartments, teenagers out of the trees. Everyone is in the street now, they surround and overturn the police vans, kick down the barricades. The boys with the huge speakers in the backs of their cars have been waiting years for this; they throw open all the doors and windows and crank the bass. The coolers in the delis are empty already, they're raiding the basements, holding up delivery trucks, the gutters run bubbly with beer.

Lucas is too weak to stand. He kneels in front of his apartment building, his robes in sooty tatters. Diane crouches, throws her arms around him, kisses the back of his neck, almost knocks him over, but Inspector Trout steadies him. He heard what Lucas said to Wendell, feels the shadow in the sky pass over him, prepares himself to believe. The party is only yards away and the noise makes the Arabs in Bay Ridge turn their heads and wonder, but Wendell can't hear it; there is only Lucas's voice, and what it can tell him about his baby.

"Where is he?" Wendell says.

One year seven months ago: snow caps the tops of the projects, the scrappy lawns around them are thick with it, the walkways unshoveled. On the steep streets in Highbridge, the cold cracks the pavement, takes chips off decaying apartment buildings. On the avenues and the intersections under the subway, the comidas típicas with neon blinking through steamed windows are closing, they're turning off the heat lamps over the yucca, wrapping themselves in thin coats, thin scarves, running home. The streets are lined with humps of white, the snow on the street unsullied by the tires of half-rusted tow trucks, ambulances, desperate gypsy cabs; the sidewalk has a tight groove in it from where the last kids trudged back to their rooms, the rooms of others, the corners of lobbies. Steam heat rattles and bangs in the pipes, sends a hot damp through old places; on the top floors, a man opens the windows a crack, crouches by the sill, smoking. The homeless freeze to death on the riverbank, get sick in the shelters and flophouses, toss in dirty sheets. Even the expressways that maimed and amputated these neighborhoods are quiet; a few trucks growling over ice, their drivers peering through wipers loaded with slush into the flurried air three feet in front of them. So only two people, walking arm in arm along 132nd Street by the warehouses, boarded-up strip clubs, and train tracks see the pod streak down from the sky on a stripe of light and rocket into the Harlem River, punching through the thin ice in a blossom of waves and steam. They stop, wait; a minute later, it bubbles to the surface, eddies, tangles in rope and electrical wire snarled along the shore—

Lucas says: "There was a survivor of that crash, but it was very hurt. In pieces. Agitated. At first they thought it was just the pain, but then they understood later, when it was able to put itself back together, that it was trying to tell them something—"

"—Them?" Wendell says.

"Your lover, Mr. Manuel Rodrigo de Guzmán González," Lucas says, "and Lavinia, the wife of El Flaco."

Out on the runway of JFK, the Ecuadorians notice a shift in flight patterns. Planes are being grounded, planes are being recalled, rerouted. The workers with headphones to the control tower are running for the terminal. The Ecuadorians blink, staring upward. The sky is a bright dead sphere, the middle of the ocean; but then something unfocuses the sun, makes it bleary. The memory of the Cuchumantanes, the vertical fields of corn and beans, rises in each of them, and they know without having to speak that they are all thinking the same thing.

One year three months ago. The crash survivor is kept in a dilapidated warehouse in Mott Haven, where the trains from the suburbs leap over the streets. Manuel and Lavinia visit it at night, take the subway up to the shuttered diners and run along 138th Street, where the people know Manuel by sight, know better than to ask him what he's doing. He intimates that anyone who follows him flirts with castration. The boys in front of the tire shop on the corner believe him, after what he did to an assassin sent by El Flaco, they believe him. But they notice things. First it is just him and Lavinia, or him alone; but soon it's him and a few men they do not recognize, men who look terrified to be in the South Bronx. There are five of them now. Manuel. Lavinia. A doctor. An engineer. And the man who would become the Church's High Epopt, who, by insisting on going to the warehouse, doomed himself to immolation on a water tower.

The doctor does not have to know anything about the alien's physiology to know that its health is deteriorating. Its auto-reconstruction after the crash, it seems, was not complete, something went wrong, and now there are massive infections. Visible growths of bacteria colonies, patches of fungus. The alien oozes a yellow substance from its joints that smells like rotting pork marinated in frankincense. It gurgles, draws diagrams on a giant piece of plywood. Schematics for machinery, says the engineer; but then he takes it back. It's a horoscope chart, a star map. The alien's head droops, the limbs curl and crackle. The humans look at each other. They don't get it.

"That was how the Church started," Lucas says. "They let people in one by one, people who might understand what it was trying to tell them. It was so desperate. It kept showing them pictures. Something was coming this way, they knew that. The alien traced the skyline of the city in chalk on the warehouse floor, then obliterated it with its foot. A meteor, they thought, like what happened to the dinosaurs. A meteor could do that. But no, no."

Robert Lord Townsend, Jr., is at yet another board meeting. A flabby man in a wrinkled suit is explaining their life insurance policies, but Robert is staring at the fishbowl view of the city below, the sprawl of metal, glass, and concrete. It is getting darker; he assumes it is a coming storm, something swelling up from the south, or roaring down from the north. He regrets his lack of an umbrella, and thinks, by association, of Ma Xiao Ling. It is not only umbrellas that remind him of her: car alarms, black suede shoes, the taste of cinnamon, and white pigeons also summon her. He constructs elaborate fantasies of him and her in which all of these are involved. In his latest, they are walking through a park in the rain; the umbrella is a glowing pink, she is wearing the shoes, the pigeons are nestling under sopping benches. A single car alarm cycles through its sirens, far away, muffled by water. The cinnamon is on her cheek.

Twenty-three. Twenty-two.

Eleven months ago. The alien balloons from infection. Ooze keeps pouring from cracks in its skin, the yellow contaminated with strains of green and black. The scent of frankincense weakens, is replaced by the odor of rancid peas and onions. For two days, a leg swings from the torso in spasms; then it falls off. The doctor has no idea what to do, administers morphine. Her patient gives no sign that it has done any good. Forty-six hours later, it emits a burbling cry, shudders, and changes color; then one of the appendages on its head detaches itself, rolls down the bulbous carcass. It does not move again.

The embryonic Church does not know what to do with it. They heave it into the back of a stolen ambulance, drive it to a glassmaking factory, where they attempt to incinerate it. Its head explodes when the temperature reaches boiling, but the rest of the body just heats up, steams and bubbles for four hours. They leave the ambulance by the razor-wired cyclone fence of a scrap yard, steal a truck, and drive the corpse to the bridge over Hell Gate. They have heard that the currents used to pull ships to the bottom and keep them there, that things lost in Hell Gate are never found. It is four in the morning, and almost no one is on the bridge: a dairy truck, a tractor-trailer loaded with furniture. Three tiny Japanese cars with tinted windows, racing stripes, and oversized engines roar by, weaving from lane to lane, unaware how close they come to an accident that kills them all. The members of the Church lose sight of the body as soon as it is over the edge; they do not even hear it enter the water.

The drawings remain. The pieces of plywood, the chalk markings on the floor. The stacks of notebooks and reams of paper written by the Church members trying to decipher the alien's message. There are twenty-seven people in the Church now and they are all working on them, but only the High Epopt and the engineer are making any progress. The ship sleeps under a green canvas tarp in the warehouse basement, surrounded by a phalanx of rat traps, a ring of poison. It is the province of the engineer alone. He stays in the basement for days at a time, trying to make it work. Six times he has come very close to detonating whatever makes the ship run. He calculates that if he hadn't averted the explosion, he would have put a hole in the South Bronx and rerouted the Harlem River. He emerges only to eat runny eggs and white toast at the diner near the train tracks, as job and apartment slip away from him. The boys at the tire shop see him come and go, come and go. They want to ask him what he is up to, but don't; they are afraid of him.

"The engineer had been at NASA," Lucas says. "He had seen hints of what was coming. He read a story into the numbers, and made the mistake of being too persistent about explaining them to government officials. They sent him in for a psychiatric evaluation, suggested he take some time off. He accepted their offer. They did not realize he would never come back.

"But he could not make sense of the data by himself. Its conclusion was too strange, too far outside of what he had been trained to accept, and at the same time, it shared too much with the things he had dreamt as a child. It took the High Epopt to push him there, back to that place in his head, or what was left of that place after the ravages of scientific training. Together they could understand. A scientist and a man of apocalyptic faith, they had the balance of rigor and credulity that led to the sussing out of unbelievable things."

The sunlight dissipates, turns the water of Jamaica Bay from blue to gray, but the ocean has been picking up vibrations for days, and Swami Horowitz reads the signs on the waves. He watches the shore birds gather in the tall grasses and take off, heading south, heading north. Heading away. The schools of fish are leaving, the water around and under the house is empty. The crab catch has dwindled. Everything is going, and Swami Horowitz does not know why. But he always said he would not be caught unprepared again, he has said it for decades. He goes into his parents' closet and retrieves a red metal fire ax. Swinging it over his shoulder, he walks to the set of ropes and wooden planks connecting his house to the land and hacks it to pieces. When the last rope flies apart, the house shudders, bobs, but Swami Horowitz has been thorough: it rights itself and is floating sure, moving into deeper water. He climbs to the roof, unlashes the masts and fixes them in place. Then he unfurls the sails, and soon he is heading for open water under a strong wind. He has a shotgun, he has canned goods. He has nets to fish. He looks back at the city he loves, the rising towers and low houses already receding, growing hazy in smog and distance. I will come back, he thinks, but only after. Let calamity pass over me and go. I and the planet will abide.

"You are talking about an invasion," Inspector Trout says.

"Any place with over a million people, it seems," Lucas says, and he makes a gesture with his hand that suggests smoothing over. "And there are ten million people here. At least."

"For almost a year you knew about this and told nobody?" Masoud says.

"I was not yet in the Church," Lucas says. "But they tried. Nobody would believe them. The authorities did not understand the diagrams and would not suffer their explanation. A few of the early ones were committed to institutions. And why not? We have no evidence. Without these," he waves toward the bodies of the Horsemen, the limbs of which are still squirming toward their torsos, preparing for reattachment, "no rational person would believe."

"You had the body," Inspector Trout says.

"Had it. But we had put it in the river."

"You had the ship."

Nineteen. Eighteen.

"No. We lost it. Wendell, please forgive him."

Three months ago: an argument, the first schism in the Church of Panic. We have to keep trying to explain it, the High Epopt says. The ship is the proof, its machinery is like nothing anyone has ever seen. It proves there is something here. It and the diagrams. Someone will be convinced.

But the machinery doesn't work, the engineer says. If no one can see it in motion, we won't convince anyone. We're just fifty-eight lunatics with a complicated movie prop and some schematics so dense and unintelligible that they show all the signs of paranoid schizophrenia. People are locked away for much less.

"But we have to try," the High Epopt says.

"See you in the asylum," the engineer says.

The truth is that idea of the impending invasion is driving them all a little mad. It is too much to bear, the scale of it, its mass. Knowing the date. None of them can sleep, they have trouble eating. Almost all of them have lost their jobs: too distracted, unwilling to say why. Some of them have thought about fleeing the country, going to a town with seven people in it in the Adirondacks, no, no, to Zambia, or the Amazon Basin, or an uninhabited island in the South Pacific, there must be some of those left, right? The Outback. The Sahara Desert, Antarctica, Mongolia, Siberia, there's nobody in Siberia anymore. The Arctic Circle. But they know the invasion is only the first step, there are successive phases that seem to involve a sort of slow enveloping, a spreading across the globe, tendrils connecting city to city, then off-shoots from those, iterating and growing denser until the planet is covered.

The ship does not work, the engineer repeats. Pity him, the wretch, for he is lying. Four months ago, he managed at last to turn it on; a low green light flowed from the interior, a high whir, controls he did not know were there budded from panels and wrapped themselves around his arms. They were awaiting instructions, that much was clear. Back to the drawings, the diagrams. He trolled through his memories, revisiting movements and noises the alien had made when it seemed cogent. For three weeks, it was just the engineer and the unmoving ship, him dancing and singing inside it, swamped in a frustration festering into desperation. The ship all serene patience. At three forty-two in the morning one night, he got the ship to move, but it was all mistakes: he lurched it into the wall, smacked it into the ceiling. Then, for another week, a controlled hover, the barest movement. He was beginning to understand it, at least how to use it. He hauled it with a forklift into the chasm of the warehouse one night, turned it on, brought it to a float. It did not make a sound beyond that same high whir, emitted no fumes. He made it kiss the walls, nudge the ceiling, move through the warehouse space; then he opened the loading doors and flew it to the roof, parked it there, covered it with a tarp. The next night, a small trip over the neighborhood, generating calls to the police from panicked neighbors that went uninvestigated. At last, a trip from

New York to Nebraska and back again that took four minutes without taxing the engines. The ship worked; as far as he knew, it was in perfect condition.

The engineer and the High Epopt stare at each other.

"We can't just leave everyone to die," the High Epopt says. It is the last move he has.

"We don't have any choice," the engineer says. He is so good at lying that the High Epopt, who prides himself on understanding men, detects nothing. A groan escapes him, he almost chokes on it; then he turns and leaves the warehouse, nods at the tire shop boys, and takes the subway to 103rd Street. He does not know what else to do. People are coming to the Mayhem Seat in fours and fives, accountants, waitresses, men from the Midwest with freckles and dirty blond hair, boys from East New York with lopsided afros who saw something over their apartment building and knew it wasn't the weed. A woman from Alaska, who noticed the shift in wind patterns, fluctuations in the weather. An amateur astronomer, who saw it through his telescope two weeks ago, after a sudden storm had taken the humidity away. We've seen the signs in the sky, they say. We can't carry this by ourselves. There are hundreds of people in the Church now, crossing the city in threes, trying to tell people what is coming. New converts approach them at bus stops, the entrances to subway stations, they chase them down the street and tug at their robes. Tell me how I can escape. Tell me there's some way to fight it. Tell me there's something I can do.

That night the engineer takes a ten-hour walk by the warehouses and projects, the hulks of schools, the leaning fences of abandoned lots and construction that's been half-finished for years. He walks under the elevated trains, over University Heights Bridge into Upper Manhattan, by the vendors hawking coffee in thermoses to drivers who pretend to ignore them, then roll down the window just long enough to let a dollar slip out, let a paper cup come in. He walks through Inwood to Washington Heights, past the graffiti on the gated stores on 207th, down Broadway, the look on his face immunizing him from crime. The light in El Flaco's office is on, but he knows El Flaco is not there, knows his wife is.

"The ship works," he tells her.

"Where will we go?" she says.

"Does it matter?"

". . ."

"It can fit three," the engineer says.

One month ago. She tells Manuel they are leaving in thirty-six hours. Come with us, she says. I don't want to go without you, but I'm not staying here. We deserve this, she says. We found it, you and I, and we deserve it.

Thirty-five hours later, he is lying on the pier at Coney Island, wracked by chemicals, staring at the sky. The Russians are singing the old songs and playing the accordion. The rides are closing down for the night, bells and hammers, buzzers and chimes tiring out, dying away. Children hold Mylar balloons, fathers with mustaches and sunglasses and mothers in tank tops amble behind them; today is their day off, they worked three months straight for it and are determined to use every last minute, they'll watch day turn to night here and kiss after the child has fallen asleep, kiss and speak like they did when they were young. All along the beach, the lights are coming on and the sky is going dark. And in the space of a second, Manuel Rodrigo de Guzmán González leaps to his feet, sprints to the end of the pier, vaults over the railing, limbs flailing, and plummets toward the purple water; but he never reaches it. To those that see him go, it is like he vanished in midair. They do not believe it. They scan the water for the man who isn't there, who is already far above them, and then do not speak of it, not to anyone. Except maybe in their sleep: the words mumble from a confused brain that he disappeared halfway down and was gone. Poof.

"They took the ship and left us," Lucas says. "They left us with nothing but the charts and diagrams that only we understood. Our knowledge. Our faith."

The party on Van Brunt has reached an epic size; half of the partiers have no idea why they're there, never saw the attacks of the Horsemen on the news, they're just there to drink and dance, to move their bodies, to look at women. Salmon is fighting through this pulsing crowd, trying to find Trout, for someone at last relayed Dr. Gore's message to him and he has put it together, he understands and he needs more than anything to talk to his partner, to put a frame around the tentacled idea in his head.

"The Four Horsemen came after they left, looking for the one who warned us. Of course, it was long dead by the time they got here, but that did not prevent them, I do not know how, from finding out what it had done. They must have followed the connections, from the ship to Manuel and Lavinia; from Manuel to you, Wendell; then from Manuel to the

Church of Panic. From there, it is only natural that they learned we had everything the alien had ever given us."

"But you do not understand what it gave you," Trout says.

"It's almost comic, isn't it?" Lucas says. "They must have feared the worst, that the alien had managed to explain everything, that we had comprehended at once, and that we were capable of mobilizing against them. They must have feared finding a planet in arms, organized, prepared to resist. But they only found us, half-deranged insomniacs with plans we cannot fathom." Lucas laughs now, a strange and uncomfortable cackle that turns heads, but he composes himself. "No. All we ever learned was that they were coming. And we learned when."

"And that is."

Four. Three. Two.

"Right now."

CHAPTER ∞

In Which Unbelievable Events Occur

 Visitors

It begins with ribbons of light that curl down from the sky, turning in eddies of wind, lacing through rasps of cloud, and at last, weaving through the buildings of Manhattan, a fork of slow lightning that spreads over the island, reaches into the outer boroughs, and then stops, thrumming. The first ships come down, they move through weather patterns, shafts of smog and steam, the spaces between skyscrapers, the diesel air over apartments, like giant beetles, chirping at each other and wavering. They stop and hold position, over the hundreds of streets, with millions of people staring up at them in awe.

The city is quiet for the first time in two centuries. Cars have stopped, phones have been hung up, put away, street musicians damp their strings. The arguments and clack of chess pieces in parks, the drunks jabbering on cyclone fences, the radios in photograph-slathered apartments, the kids on the sidewalk with broom handles chasing rats, the vendors hawking knockoffs, the old men in tank tops sitting on lawn chairs, the spin of Laundromats, frying food, the clatters of subways on the elevated tracks—all has stopped. Then the noise really begins: a guttural rumble that starts as far-off thunder and becomes a squadron of planes, but keeps growing, a sound so loud and deep that buildings sway and heave, windows shatter; then the clouds part over New York and an impossible object half again as long as Manhattan descends, stops two hundred feet from the top of the Empire State Building. Monstrous tentacles unfold and sweep over Brooklyn and Queens, stretch long shadows over the Bronx. It hovers there in twenty-nine square miles of airspace, and its metallic shrieks carry for hundreds more.

"Ladies and gentlemen," Lucas announces, "I give you phase one of the occupation of our planet by an alien power. It is a grand time to be alive."

Robert Lord Townsend, Jr., and the board of directors are plastered against the glass, eyes trained upward at a sky of dark material, streams of light, the passage of alien craft; the shrieks rattle the roof, spill coffee, sway the floor and the fifty-two stories of office workers and equipment beneath them. There are exclamations of genteel panic, talk of being airlifted, but Robert Lord Townsend, Jr., feels the blood of his murderous ancestor rising in him, and while the others are still debating whether or not to call a helicopter, he has vaulted down eight stories of stairs, tie flapping behind him, tears appearing in the creases of his pants, and his head is focused on one thing only: to find Ma Xiao Ling, and tell her he loves her.

She is in Chinatown, her feet surrounded by a swarm of escaped crabs; someone knocked over a ten-gallon tub of them and now they're scrambling for freedom. Around her, people are starting to move, they've already clogged the subways, jammed the buses. The tourists don't know what to do. The vendors have already thrown their wares into vans, they're heading to Jersey with as many close friends as they can cram in the back. Ma Xiao Ling can see the Manhattan Bridge solid with clamoring cars as the behemoth alien craft blocks light overhead. Her neck tingles: a climate is gathering, like Tiananmen, like a party with armed bandits in Tajikistan when the beer is running low. In the air, she can taste riot.

In Spanish Harlem, they are thinking about Chiapas. The avenues are already swamped with people fleeing from downtown, suits, uniforms, expensive shoes, churning and pushing. Joaquín kisses his wife's forehead and tells her to go in the restaurant. He stands at the door with a smile under his mustache and a pistol shoved in the back of his pants, waiting for the first sign: breaking glass, a car on fire.

In Astoria, a coalition of Greeks and Lebanese has imposed order, thirty-six men move as a unit down Steinway with bullhorns in seven languages. Thank you for staying calm. But the Greeks in the cafés have switched from coffee to liquor and the Colombians are thinking about Medellín. And Daoud puts tape across the windows of his restaurant, piles chairs and tables near the door, pulls down the metal shield as three gigantic tentacles sweep above him. His mind traces the shortest way home if he abandons his car and runs.

The George Washington Bridge is packed with the rich and the young families, fleeing for their houses in the country, motels, the mountains. Out in Rego Park, the reporter is watching the news, sees the footage of the ships milling over the sky, the increasing panic of interviewed citizens; he takes *Death in the Five Boroughs* out of its drawer, staples a stack of blank pages to the back. I'm going to be busy tonight, he says. Please don't go to work, honey.

The crowds are growing in the streets through the outer boroughs; they are choking the bodegas in Manhattan. A tentacle arcs over Red Hook, and a ripple passes through the party; someone cuts the music off, there are shouts from the corners, cries of panic, and then it happens: chaos rolls out in waves, it shatters glass, starts fires, and now Van Brunt is a storm of faces and limbs, a cry rises from the throng: save us, save us. A scream tears from the giant ship above, and the people before Lucas's apartment are torn from each other. Diane is pulled from Lucas's arms, carried away in human undertow. Masoud is washed away from Wendell, he can see Captain Spaceman struggle, and then succumb; he is carried to where people are falling into the bay, where hundreds of stolen boats are trailing out to sea. Trout is trampled, but rises; he fights past the burning hardware stores, the buildings already scarred by flames lit and put out, lit and put out; halfway down Van Brunt, under a bower of flying trash and broken glass, he meets his fellow fish, who, slashed and battered and smeared with beer, has been clawing his way down from the tunnel to save him.

For a moment, neither speaks. The world's orbit slows as each looks the other over, the man he has worked with for twelve years.

"I came to find you," Salmon says over the din. "I figured it out, and I was coming to tell you."

"..."

"You thought I'd lost it for good, didn't you."

"I was just waiting for you to come around."

"Fantasist."

"Realist."

"Egghead."

"Simpleton."

"..."

"Don't leave me again," Trout says.

"Never," Salmon says.

The riots continue until dawn. Great fires consume seventeen city blocks, the smoke wavering up through the cloud of helicopters and their frantic searchlights to where the alien ships hover in silence. All across the city, men and women return home, to their husbands, wives, and lovers, all blood and fierce limbs. Three hundred fifty-two babies are born that night; six thousand more are conceived.

The Fall of New York

In the morning, the ships are still there, emitting chirps and low whistles; below them, the National Guard has imposed order. Jeeps heavy with uniforms patrol empty streets. Stoplights cycle. Here and there a deli is open, the owner stands behind the counter, peering out the window. Furtive citizens hurry across intersections, staring up at the small craft, the tentacles, the bulbous hulk hovering above them. We must evacuate at once, the mayor says. It is dangerous to be here, the governor says. We could not bear the loss of all your lives. But nobody will leave.

Three men are in Washington Heights, playing dominoes in a cardboard box top, underneath a patrol ship.

"Ain't nobody driving me out of my place," one man says. "It's rent-controlled."

"They want it so bad, they can come and get it," another says.

"This is my home. This is where I live. Where else can I go?" It echoes from building to building, block to block, neighborhood to neighborhood, all that fear from above beaten into the shape of pride. They want to be here for this. I was there during the riots, they'll say. I was there when the aliens came. This is who I was. This is what I did.

The second day, the bureaucracy remembers that someone had tried to warn them. The two institutionalized members of the Church of Panic are released from Bellevue, are taken in for extensive interviews with the Department of Defense. They are in there for hours, reeling off the little they understand, and the government officials at first take notes, then rely on the tape recorder, and at last are staring at them slack-jawed. They had no idea it could get so bad. Someone leaks it to the news: attacks imminent, the papers say. Death toll estimated at eight hundred thousand to eight million. Within four days. There are more pleas to flee, but everyone ignores them.

Lucas is interviewed at the request of the government. The ones you put in prison know more, he says, and besides, you owe them. On his rooftop, he finds candy wrappers that Wendell and Masoud left there; he realizes then that they were waiting for days, while he ran for his life. He sits on the dusty tar of his rooftop. The sun is setting between the alien craft and the far hills of New Jersey, and sets the water on fire. Big warships are moving into the harbor, sounding blasts across the bay; skiffs bob in their wakes, three Greenpoint boys are gathered around a cooler full of beers by the outboard motor. They're swaying in a little circle, and Lucas can hear their singing from a quarter of a mile away.

Diane ascends the fire escape and finds him there; by now, the sky has grown dark, the city lights the bottom of the ships in a luminous yellow glow, while low-flying clouds catch in its upper spires. His back is to her; she lays her fingers on his shoulder, sits next to him, close.

"..."

"..."

"How are the Ecuadorians?" Lucas says.

"They're going back. Not running away, of course, just going back, for their friends and families. The people they love. They're bringing guns and mortars. Crates and crates of shells. I don't know where they got all of it, but they got it. If they're quick, they'll be in Ecuador before the day after tomorrow, before . . ."

"Do you still love them?" Lucas says.

"Of course I do. But I've never fallen out of love with anyone, ever. Even when we've gone away from each other."

" . . . "

"It's going to be really bad, isn't it."

Lucas nods. Then: "The estimate in the paper is conservative. Eight hundred thousand is laughable, it . . . sorry."

"No. Tell me. I want to know."

"It is not just the death, death by the millions, it . . . it is said that when the Romans defeated Carthage, they did not leave one stone atop another. They salted the earth so that nothing of use could grow there again. It is said that during the civil war in Guatemala, entire towns disappeared, their people were destroyed, the houses razed and buried, the names erased from the map, so that when the refugees returned, they found only a clearing that the jungle had already half reclaimed. I tell you it will be terrible here, and you imagine half-toppled skyscrapers, corpses piled in the street, the rivers fresh with blood. But it will be far more complete than that. All this, all these people, will be a stained, sandy spit, the ocean rising to reclaim it, with that behemoth still hovering overhead, screeching and chirping. It will appear as if the city were never here at all, as if none of it had happened, all that history. All the things that people did and tried to do. It will seem as if they never were."

"..."

"It was bound to happen sooner or later, wasn't it? The fall of New York, it had to come eventually." Lucas says. "I just wish I wasn't here to see it."

"..."

"Still, I am ready. My upbringing, my beliefs, they prepared me for this."

"You know what they didn't prepare you for?" Diane says.

"No."

"Me." She turns to him, and, smiling, she kisses him on the eyes, on the nose, on the forehead, puts her hands on his chest and pushes him down onto the dust of the roof; under the tentacles, under the ships calling to each other in the yellow gloom, she reaches down and begins to pull her dress over her head.

"Death," she says, "in every moment, death by the millions is being averted. For this reason, every party must be of the highest quality."

And it is.

 Spaceman Blues

Van Brunt has been kicked in, burned out. Storefronts without windows yawn, the corners writhe with upended garbage cans bent in half, surrounded by trash. Streetlamps tilt at crazy angles, bowing into the street, reeling back into the buildings behind them. Two stoplights have been pulled down, and they lie on their sides in their intersections. One still makes the rounds from green to yellow to red; the other's lights are dark, dead. People are sleeping where they fell on stoops and corners, on beds of crumbled glass; small fires still smolder on the sidewalks, greasy smoke slides above the rooftops, where a patrol ship hovers in a quiet whir, under a vast tentacle that sweeps back and forth, exposing the street to burning sun, then thick shadow.

An alien finger is crawling along the curb, trailing fluid, calling out for the hand it came from. The hand is eighteen blocks away, lying on a storm drain; the arm is floating in the bay. When the party turned to riot, a mob set themselves to tearing apart the limbs, heads, and torsos of the Four Horsemen, and are scattering their remnants still: there are pieces on buses in Queens, on subway platforms in East Harlem. Three of the feet have ended up in shoeboxes thrown into closets, where they kick at their prisons. Two of the heads and torsos have been cut into tiny pieces and thrown off the top of a project, are lodged now in trees, park benches, and playground equipment, to be eaten by dogs and scavenging birds. Some of the fragments have managed to find their mates: here, an elbow has formed in a sheet of broken plaster, there a foot lies on its side. It will take them almost a month to reassemble, and some will never be whole again; when they return to their ship, they will be unwilling to fly sorties, unwilling even to fix machinery. After eight days of noncompliance, they will be sent home with the returning supply ships to retire in disgrace and exhaustion, to the shores of a purple ocean, catching long, four-tailed fish, sleeping under the three moons, feeling the layers of their lives settle. No more fighting for them; only rest.

Wendell wakes from dreamless sleep, crumpled in crackling plastic. There are cuts on his head, welded shut with dried blood. His limbs ache, but move; he presses his hands to his rib cage, where his heart insists on pushing blood through him, his lungs demand to draw air, stubborn, angry. He hates them for that. He considers assaulting the patrol ship above him, taking them by surprise, dismembering crew and wrecking machines, before they regroup and incinerate him. But the impulse is greater still to surrender. He does not know how he would communicate it, but there must be some way to let them know that he has had enough. He will approach the ship at night, a slow walk in full view, arms out. Take me in. Put me away. Bring me into your metal arms and throw me across space. I want to go, really I do. This place has had enough of me, now that my baby's gone away.

He stirs the plastic, rises, paces, from the corner of the deli to the fallen streetlight to the ruined mesh of the trash can in front of what used to be a hairdresser's. There, he finds the severed head of one of his enemies, whole; the rioters must have forgotten to cube it. He draws his machete and moves to chop it in half, but a grimace from it stops him. Nine years. Nine years the creature spent pulling through inky space to reach this place. It saw suns fall together, merge and explode in the brilliance of dying nebulae beyond; saw planets wheel out of orbit and freeze to death, or draw spirals of fire in their descent toward their mother star. It saw three ships fail, disintegrate in flight, thousands of its brethren tossed unprotected into vacuum; was almost lost twice itself to the work of stray debris, meteorites. It lay awake for days at a time, petrified of instant death, watched the same fear drive friends to murder and suicide, and at last overcame it, became something stronger. But now it lies scattered on a scrap-strewn pavement, calling in vain to arms and legs that are distant from it, a torso that cannot reply, for the organs are confused. They lie, nerve endings screaming and wriggling on the hard ground, searching blind for pieces that are gone far away.

The head tilts and slithers. Wendell and the alien regard each other. An understanding passes between them.

Darling, my darling. Why did you leave me to this?

There's Always a Party Somewhere

The last refugees, the ones who change their minds, fly across the bridges at ninety miles an hour, losing possessions out the window that open in a fan behind them and drop into the river. In the city, a recklessness courses through the young, there are suicides and accidents, tremendous parties, spontaneous weddings, professions of love. But the mourning has already begun: for the people that remain, the city is husband, wife, their love will not let them leave it while it is dying. They will hold its hand during its final days, and when it breathes its last, there will be no consoling them. There are people sobbing on their stoops, touching the walls and sidewalks, people doing drawings, taking photographs of the good places for tacos and beers, the gas station where their friends loitered in the summer, the corner where she kissed you, the stretch of brownstones where you let him go. It is too much, too much too fast. New York, Gotham, New Amsterdam, what will we do without you?

Behind a Laundromat in Fort Hamilton, Wendell descends into Darktown down a flight of musty stairs, to a ladder made of chains, to a landing of milk crates lapped by oily water. There he puts himself on a barge going south, tucks himself between wooden boxes filled with chickens and axle grease.

Darktown is a frenzy of activity: those who left have been replaced, by refugees from the surface, by entrepreneurs from elsewhere, trading in ammunition and medical supplies, landmines, army rations, surface-to-air missiles, blankets, water purifiers, motion detectors, radar equipment. For people who can move things, like El Flaco, business has never been better. In the market, Dr. Ease's Drug Emporium is as packed as ever, the small men are selling off cases of rum and whiskey, bags of cocaine and pills, as fast as they can put them out. It's goods from Eastern Europe, clothes from Mauritius and Sri Lanka. The rich have pulled their hands out of the market, cordoned themselves off in bunkers, and their poorer competitors, who have been waiting for this, rise to take their spots: with the imminent collapse of currency, they're using their cash for kindling, and bartering like fiends.

A passenger sitting across from Wendell is peering at him.
"You're Captain Spaceman, aren't you," he says.

". . ."

"They say you took down the Four Horsemen almost
without help. Is that true? I lost a lot of money because of you
that day. No offense, but I didn't think you stood a chance—"

"—Who are you talking about?" another passenger says.

"This here is Captain Spaceman," says the first.

"No shit? Did you really take them out with a chain saw?"

"Circular saws, you idiot. Guy who was there told me it
was like the circus up there, the way this guy moved. Circular
saws and a machete."

"No shit . . ."

"Hey, Captain," says a third, "they say you know how to
stop the invasion. That you've got a plan for bringing the big
ship down. That right? How are you going to bring it down,
though, without crushing the city underneath it? Did you
think of that?"

"Man," says a fourth, "like, I saw you on Van Brunt, man.
That was amazing, what you pulled . . ."

"You know how to beat them, right? Pull them out of the
sky?"

"People are saying you've been in the big ship, you stole
some of their secrets and that's how you beat the Horsemen—"

"—They say you know their language, Captain. They say
you know them best—"

"—Well, I don't!" Wendell shouts. "I didn't want to be a
part of all this, I was just looking for . . ."

"Captain—"

"—Please," he says, in a voice that silences them, "please just leave me alone."

There are others that recognize him, others that want to speak to him, shake his hand, look him over, the man who beat the Horsemen, who is enshrined in Hyrvygeena's walls, who is growing into a story told to children: don't worry, they say, we have someone to protect us. He wants none of it. He leaps from the barge to another one passing, vaults through it and to the other side of the canal before the driver can berate him; he flits through darkened matrices on foot now, swings from roof to roof on tethers, and returns to the place he might find a measure of peace.

When they left the suspended tugboat, the Ciphers erased every trace of their existence. The galley is scrubbed empty. The walls and floors are barren. Blank portholes stare into stark rooms. Two families live on the deck, one fore and one aft. They have no idea who lived there before and do not recognize their visitor. So Captain Spaceman goes to the hold to sleep, but he lies there instead for hours in the dim gloom of a delirium that will not slip into slumber.

"Captain—," a voice says.

"—Go away."

"Wendell. It is Masoud. I have been in Darktown all this time. I have gone from one end to the other, from Hyrvygeena to the market and back again, looking for you, or word of you."

". . ."

"They are preparing for the worst here," Masoud says. "You should see the arsenal they have. It is better than Syria's.

I am showing them how to use much of the equipment, but some of it I do not know. It is too new."

"I thought you were a pacifist."

"I was. But a man must change with the times, do you not think so?"

"..."

"You understand that was a joke? You of all people, who have changed so much—" He begins laughing, is unable to continue.

"..."

"Ahhhh ..."

"..."

"... You know that they are looking for you, because you beat the—"

"—Yes, yes, I know—"

"—Ah." Masoud says. "I suspected you would not be interested." In the halo of his flashlight, he frowns.

"What are you saying?"

"You do not think I know you by now? It is as if, halfway through his jihad, the Mahdi had been told Allah had fled Heaven. That he had been fighting for a god who abandoned him. I cannot imagine what that is like."

"..."

"You have changed so much—"

"—Look, I know what you're going to say. I'm a fighter now. See how strong I've grown. I have a fire in me now that would have killed me two months ago. But let me tell you what I want. I want to erase my name from every paper, delete my face from every memory, and—"

"—And vanish?"

"Yes! Yes!"

"But you cannot do that, Wendell. Not now. Not with what the world is going to be like."

"Why not?"

"Because we need you."

Wendell is cocked in a pose of rage, it twists his face to a look that Masoud recognizes from his dreams, on his brother, half-eviscerated, charging three machine gunners and an armored car, all hopelessness and raving anger, lobbing grenades and emptying his pistol. His ferocity kills two of the gunners before the car finishes him, and Masoud cannot wake himself before it is over.

But Wendell crumples instead, he coughs out sobs and his hands clutch his chest as if he might explode.

"But it's so hard . . . ," Wendell says.

"Yes," Masoud says. "It is."

Wendell closes his eyes. The cavern below seems to fill with brine, it sets the tugboat to floating again. The walls warp around him, the ceiling peels open to the city above. Buildings bow and swing back, the island buckles beneath them, and now the coastline arcs in, the sea swells up to receive us all, the sky shatters and collapses, and Wendell can hear the voices of millions of people, all of us, rising up to meet him in an aching dissonance, we want so much for us and the ones we love, we wring our pasts and futures from the things we've lost and the things we will never have. But then the chaos converges, six billion hearts pause and shudder to land on the same beat, a great One. The planet tilts and spins onto a new axis, weather patterns swirl and recombine, the moon slips closer and tides shift, the land rises and falls, drawing air into the lungs of the world that will survive long after the aliens have taken what they want and abandoned us, long after we've gone, until the sun swells and devours us. The One drops. All is still. Then it passes, and a new measure begins, the planet slips back into orbit, the moon resumes its old course, the patient oceans subside. The water draws out of Darktown, leaving its people drenched and bewildered. The tugboat sways in the air twice more and stops; in the dark hold, Wendell is cradled in Masoud's arms, and he opens his eyes just soon enough to realize that Masoud has put a kiss on his forehead; a benediction, a sign.

"Come," he says. "Come and join us. There are people who do not want to die tomorrow, who will make something out of even this. There are parties tonight, music, dancing. The good things in life. Other men. Other women. Come, brother, and join us."

Tonight, on the eve of invasion, there will be parties all across the city. Bands will play until their fingers break open and bleed, until their lips split, until their throats run out of speech; people will dance, hands in the air, arms around each other, until their legs give out and they buckle over in ecstasy. The air will taste sweet tonight, the sky will riot with fire under the dark ship, for these people are the lucky ones, the ones who saw it and survived. And Wendell will go with them; he will begin to cut the strings that lash him to the one he loved and who left him behind. He will find himself here, in a dark place with music and a thousand friendly strangers, and he will begin to pull from the ground, from the water, from the atmosphere of this lunatic planet, the feeling that left him two months, four days, and seven hours ago, when his baby, his Manuel, his only, flew away. It will not come yet, but it is coming soon. We promise.

Happiness.

Wendell's Dream #4

The city is on fire; glass explodes, asphalt melts, brick and stone crack and crumble, the fire sweeps across the earth, flows up the sides of collapsed buildings, tendrils into the sky, wavering into black smoke until the air stinks of tar and copper. Wendell is high above it all in a hot air balloon of many colors with an octopus who plays the violin, a slow, sweet melody that Wendell does not know.

"What song is that?" Wendell says.

The octopus shrugs. "Something I made up. I don't know what it is yet."

"Does it have a name?"

"Nope."

Below them, the foundations of a huge tower melt away at last, and with a groan of girders the spire topples sideways, crushing other buildings beneath it. Flames crawl over all.

"What," says Wendell.

"You're supposed to jump."

"But there's a fire down there."

The octopus stops playing. "Look. I know a lot of songs, but you're supposed to jump."

"..."

"Jump already."

Wendell puts one hand on the edge of the basket and leaps over it. He tumbles end over end between the walls of heat and noise. The flames below him go out in a huff of breath and the ground parts; he is falling through cool air toward a multitude singing and dancing and setting off fireworks. They do not see his descent, so he calls out to them one by one, all their names and the places they were born. They all look up at the same time, a collective shout of recognition flies into Wendell's ears, and a million hands rise to catch him.

ACKNOWLEDGMENTS

To my wife, Stephanie, who told me a couple of years ago that she would be mad if I stopped writing, and then told me how to do it better. To Liz Gorinsky, my editor at Tor, who made this happen. To the many, many musicians, living and dead, who taught me how I wanted to play. To New York City.

Many of the locations in the book were inspired by actual places. Those who are interested in going to these places are encouraged to contact me. I should be easy to find.

12366823R00142

Made in the USA
Lexington, KY
06 December 2011